Lure

*10 Colborne Street, built in 1851 for
Mrs. Helen Ramsden, née Frizzell. It was converted in
1960 into the Thornhill Village Library.*

Lure

Deborah Kerbel

DUNDURN PRESS

TORONTO

Editor: Shannon Whibbs
Design: Jennifer Scott
Printer: Webcom

Library and Archives Canada Cataloguing in Publication

Kerbel, Deborah
        Lure / by Deborah Kerbel.

Also available in electronic format.
ISBN 978-1-55488-754-5

        I. Title.

PS8621.E75L87 2010   jC813'.6   C2010-902307-2

1   2   3   4   5   14   13   12   11   10

 Conseil des Arts   Canada Council   Canadä   ONTARIO ARTS COUNCIL
du Canada   for the Arts   CONSEIL DES ARTS DE L'ONTARIO

We acknowledge the support of the **Canada Council for the Arts** and the **Ontario Arts Council** for our publishing program. We also acknowledge the financial support of the **Government of Canada** through the **Canada Book Fund** and **The Association for the Export of Canadian Books**, and the **Government of Ontario** through the **Ontario Book Publishers Tax Credit** program, and the **Ontario Media Development Corporation**.

Care has been taken to trace the ownership of copyright material used in this book. The author and the publisher welcome any information enabling them to rectify any references or credits in subsequent editions.

J. Kirk Howard, President

Printed and bound in Canada.   www.dundurn.com

Dundurn Press
3 Church Street, Suite 500
Toronto, Ontario, Canada
M5E 1M2

Gazelle Book Services Limited
White Cross Mills
High Town, Lancaster, England
LA1 4XS

Dundurn Press
2250 Military Road
Tonawanda, NY
U.S.A. 14150

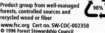 **Mixed Sources**
Product group from well-managed forests, controlled sources and recycled wood or fiber
www.fsc.org Cert no. SW-COC-002358
© 1996 Forest Stewardship Council
FSC

 **ANCIENT FOREST** ™ **FRIENDLY**

For my Dad,
Who took me fishing, taught me patience,
blessed me with books, and passed me his pen.

And for my Jonah,
Who loves a good ghost story.

And for my Dahlia,
Sweet, little "me-too."

This book is based on true accounts of supernatural occurrences at the Thornhill Village Public Library.

1 – John

Of all I've had to endure over the past century, the darkness is what bothers me the most. It fills my head, clogs my eyes and ears, pins me down like a weight upon my chest. The darkness has drawn a curtain between me and the rest of the world. I can see out, but no one else can see in. The darkness has become my prison; my sentence is forever. Unless, of course, I can find someone to help release me.

But, I'm getting ahead of myself. My dear mother would have scolded me for being so rude. Of course, I should have started with an introduction.

During my brief life, my name was John McCallum. I was the fifth John to live at 10 Colborne Street. Although I wasn't born in the house, it was the core of my childhood, the witness to my awkward adolescence, and my home when this young life was cut off so suddenly — like a limp sapling severed by the gardener's shears. But although my life was short, over time my roots have grown surprisingly long and deep. They've remained with the house even after so many years have passed, after other families have come and gone, and in the years since, the building has taken on a new life of its own as a library.

Granted, I'm not the only one. There are other people with roots here. I've passed their cold souls in the hallways, heard them moaning at night, smelled their earthy scents. My own mother is one of them although, ironically, she can't seem to see my face as much as she searches for it. Yes, this house has been a magnet for the unsettled. And yet I can assure you that none of the others have an attachment to this place as strong as mine. Since my sudden passing, the walls of 10 Colborne Street have become my skin, the beams my bones, and the lingering memory of what took place here has become my life's blood.

When you walk through the doorway, tread lightly and treat me with care. For my eyes never close ... even after you've come and gone.

2 – Max

"Help! Stop that dog!"

I turned to see a small black pug dashing frantically up the road toward me, barking and yelping like it was going mad. Curious, I stopped walking and stared. There was a pretty blonde girl running behind the dog. She was yelling at the top of her voice.

"Come on, help me catch him!"

Was she talking to me? That would be a switch! Up until that moment, the only people in this crappy little suburb to speak to me had been my teachers — and they were getting paid to do that. The girl's panicked eyes met mine as she sprinted closer.

"Please ... before he gets hit by a car!"

Yup ... she's definitely talking to me. My eyes darted around, looking for cars. There were none in sight on the quiet side street where the dog was coming from. But if the little guy made it up to where I was standing on Yonge Street, I knew that nothing was going to keep him safe from the rush of the morning traffic. Thinking fast, I jogged down the road to block his path. Out of the corner of my eye, I could see the blonde girl closing in behind the pug in the hopes of cornering him. The poor dog was barking wildly as he zigzagged back and forth across the road. Although I'd never had a dog of my own, I knew enough about them to understand that this one had been badly spooked by something. He wasn't going to be easy to catch without some kind of bait. Unzipping my backpack, I reached in and pulled out my lunch bag.

Baloney ... perfect!

Ripping open the wrapper, I held the sandwich out toward the yapping dog and shook it to get his attention.

"Come here, boy! Come get a treat!" I called out in that high-pitched kind of way that dogs like. Within seconds, his flat little nose caught the scent. Suddenly, he switched direction and began running toward me.

"Good boy ... that's right. Come get your snack."

When he reached me, I gently took hold of his collar and gave him the sandwich. I could feel his body trembling beneath my fingers while he ate. Hoping to calm him, I stroked his little black head in the spot behind his ears where every dog loves to be scratched. He looked at me with his scrunched-up face and licked my arm. Moments later, the blonde girl caught up to us, gasping for breath from the chase.

"Thank you so much!" she panted, falling to her knees and hugging the dog. "Peanut's never run away like that before ... I-I don't know what happened."

I shrugged. "Well, something must have scared him. Look, he's still shaking."

She leaned over, kissed the top of his head, and cooed in his ear like he was a baby or something. I looked away. What was it with people and their little toy dogs? She wasn't one of those weirdos who liked dressing them up in those stupid outfits, was she? I turned my eyes back to look at the girl more closely. She didn't look like a weirdo. She was dressed in jeans, a light sweater, and a pair of red Chucks. She was probably a few years older than me and she wasn't wearing any make-up, but she didn't need to. She had sunny blonde hair that bounced off her shoulders and bright blue eyes. There was something about her face that was familiar. Like an actress that I'd seen in a dozen movies, but for the life of me, I couldn't remember her name.

"That was a genius idea you had there," she said to me once she was finished kissing her dog.

"What idea?"

"You know, with the sandwich? It was perfect. I wouldn't have thought of it in a million years."

A flash of embarrassed heat warmed my face. I'd just turned sixteen, but I still hadn't figured out how to take compliments from good-looking girls. "Oh … yeah, thanks," I said, picking up my backpack from the road. "Well, I better go … see ya later."

I turned back south and began dragging my feet down Yonge Street, trying to clear my head from the commotion of the past few minutes. I wasn't exactly sure if I was heading to school or not, but I tried to be cool and pretend like I knew exactly where I was going. It was late September, the sky was a cloudless blue and the air was as fresh and crisp as a ripe apple. Normally a day like that would make me feel good in a new-school-year, fresh-start kind of way. But not this one. My first year at Thornhill High School was shaping up to be the worst year of my entire life. I didn't know what was wrong with the kids in that place, but nobody had said a word to me in the three weeks since school started. Nobody! It was like I was see-through. For the millionth time since we moved here last month, I wondered why my parents had brought me to this suburban hellhole.

I only made it a few steps before I heard the girl's voice calling out from behind me.

"Wait!"

I looked back over my shoulder. She was standing in the middle of the sidewalk with the black pug by her side. Something about the look on her face reminded me of a lonely little kid searching for someone to play with.

"At least let me buy you a replacement lunch," she said, walking toward me. "There's a deli up on Centre Street that makes a fabulous submarine to go. That is, unless you have a class to get to …"

I paused to consider her offer. Truthfully, I didn't like baloney enough to care about losing the sandwich. If I went with her now to the submarine shop, I'd be late for my first class. And the idea of ditching school felt like a good one. Just so you know, ditching wasn't something I'd ever done before. Back in Vancouver, I'd been a pretty good student. But over here, the thought of being in school made me want to hurl.

"So, do you have a class to get to or not?" she asked, her shoulders curling up like question marks.

"Um, no … no class. I have a free period on Wednesday mornings," I heard myself lie. *Hunh … where'd that come from?* The girl and her dog were quickly closing the gap between us. I could hear their footsteps crunching through the fallen leaves as they approached.

"Really? Great ... so, what do you say to that sub?"

My mind spun with options.

1. Go to school and be miserable and alone.
2. Ditch classes and wander around the city alone.
3. Let the pretty blonde girl buy me lunch.

It was a total no-brainer.

"Um ... okay," I said with a nod. "Thanks."

The girl smiled and pointed her thumb back in the direction she'd just come from. "Great ... come with me for a minute and let me get my purse."

I followed her half a block down the narrow road and up the path toward a white, clapboard house. There was a sign hanging from a hook on the front. It read: *Thornhill Village Library*.

A library? *Really?* I took a closer look at the building. It had a peaked roof, green shuttered windows, and a bright red front door with an old-fashioned knocker. Truthfully, it looked more like a cottage than a library.

"What is this place?" I asked the girl. "Do you live here?"

She laughed, which totally made me wish I could take the question back. "No, I don't live here ... although sometimes after a long day of work, it can definitely start to feel that way."

Too embarrassed to look at her, I kept my eyes glued to the building. There was something peculiar about it ... like it had a story it was aching to tell. She must have noticed me staring.

"Interesting, isn't it? Ten Colborne Street was one of the first homes in Thornhill. In fact, the town has designated it a historic site." She pointed up to a round plaque on the far left side of the house. "See?"

I took a step forward so I could see it better. It read: *Mrs. Ellen Ramsden, née Frizzell. 1851.*

Wild.

"So ... this used to be a home?" I asked, finally turning my eyes back to the girl.

"Yeah, that's right. There were lots of different families who lived here over the years, but it was bought by the town and converted into a library sometime back in the sixties. My grandmother was one of the original librarians." She smiled and put a hand over her heart. "By the way, I'm Caroline."

For the first time, I noticed the little gap between her two front teeth. It was kind of quirky. I liked that. Something about this girl was so intriguing.

And it wasn't just because she was the first person to actually notice me around here. What was it about her?

She cleared her throat, bringing my thoughts racing back to the moment. "I said my name is Caroline," she repeated.

Oops!

"Sorry. I'm Max."

She tilted her head to one side, studying my face.

"Have I seen you here at the library before, Max? You look familiar."

Her eyes were such a vivid shade of blue — like forget-me-not flowers. The skin on my face was getting warm again. I glanced down at my sneakers, suddenly wondering if this sub thing was such a good idea. "Um ... no, my family just moved to Thornhill a couple of months ago. I ... I haven't met too many people yet."

That was, quite possibly, the understatement of the millennium. I'd met nobody. And nobody here seemed too eager to meet me. *It takes a while to make friends ... give it time*, my mom has been telling me at dinner every night since we got here. But how much time was I supposed to spend walking around feeling transparent? Man, why did we ever have to leave Vancouver, anyway?

"Well, now you know me," she said, striding up the winding garden path toward the side entrance of the house. "I'm very glad to meet you, Max. And so is Peanut."

I followed close behind, curious to look around the inside of the library. I'd seen lots of old buildings before ... even worked on a few with my grandfather. So, I really couldn't explain why I felt so drawn to this one. But I was. It was kind of like the thing was pulling me over to whisper a secret in my ear. As we approached the side door, the pug narrowed its eyes and started to growl. Deep, guttural, and ferocious — it was a surprisingly big sound coming from such a small animal.

"Quiet now, boy. It's all right," I heard Caroline whisper as she reached for the door handle. But Peanut clearly didn't agree with her. Before she could pull open the door, he began to bark and back away from the building. I could sense that he was only moments away from taking off again.

"Um ... call me crazy, but I don't think he wants to go in there," I said.

Ignoring me, Caroline reached down for the dog, but he scampered away from her hands and hid behind a tall cluster of daisies. She stood back up and shook her head in defeat. "Okay boy, you get your way. I guess I'll just leave you outside," she said with a sigh, turning toward me. "Sorry, Max, but would you mind watching him while I get my purse? I honestly have no idea why he's acting like this."

No idea? Really? How could she not see it?

I crouched down so I could keep an eye on Peanut and make sure he didn't run into the street again. "Sure ... but I can tell you what's wrong with your dog if you want."

Her lips pressed together, like she was trying to hold in a smile. "Oh, are you some kind of dog whisperer or something?"

I shook my head. "No, not at all. I just think it's obvious why he doesn't want to go in there."

Her lips lost the battle and widened into a big smile. "Okay, let's hear your theory," she said. But I could tell by the look on her face that she was humouring me. And her hand was still gripping the door handle, like all she wanted to do was go inside and get her purse.

"Well, it's not exactly a theory," I replied. "More of a fact, actually. Your dog is obviously terrified. Something in there must have freaked him out."

Caroline's hand floated slowly down from the door handle and her mouth fell open into a circle of surprise. "You know, you might be right about that. Something similar happened to one of the other librarian's dogs a few months ago," she said, her voice suddenly distant. "It was growling up a storm in the front parlour."

A parlour? In a library? Okay, this I had to see.

"Yeah, it was bristling and baring its teeth, like it was getting ready to fight off some kind of monster." She crossed her arms in front of her chest. It almost looked as if she was fending off a sudden chill.

"So ... what was it?" I asked.

"What was *what*?"

"You know ... the thing in the parlour that spooked the dog?"

Caroline's mouth curled up into a perfect Mona Lisa smile. "Oh yeah, that's right ... you're new around here. I guess that means you haven't heard about our ghost."

3 — John

During my brief existence, I was the only child of Elizabeth and Robert McCallum ... the only living child, that is. There were other babies — eleven to be exact. Most of them were boys, but none of them survived past the age of two. To my mother, I was a treasure — her one surviving child to be cherished and protected at all costs. Mother was one of those women who loved babies and children and always dreamed of having a large family. It was the tragedy of her life that she had only me to raise. As you might imagine, she doted on me constantly and took great pleasure in indulging my every whim.

My father, of course, hated the way she cared for me. To him, I was an endless disappointment. He never came out and said those words to me, but it was there in his cold silver eyes every morning when he glowered at my skinny body and weak appetite over the breakfast table. I sensed … no, I knew that every part of him wished one of the other sons had survived in my place. But God had chosen to taunt my iron-fisted father with weak, disease-prone children. Since all he had was me, he'd made it his life's mission to toughen my body and spirit. Unfortunately, Father had come to the conclusion that beatings were the best way to accomplish that task. And he was dedicated in his resolve.

The memories that remain of my early childhood are a patchwork of scattered events. For it was not until the arrival of William in our home that my life experiences began to take on a more solid form.

As you might imagine, my early years were quite lonely. I looked forward to school every day, as sharing the company of other children was something I craved. At the end of each school year, I was miserable at the notion of leaving my classmates, whose homes were scattered in every direction across the expanse of our village. In our home on Colborne Street, my only company was Mother and Father (aside for the daily visit from Edward the milkman, which, desperate as I was for friends, I always looked forward to). Of course, I couldn't include Kate, our hired girl, as a companion of any sort. Although she was merely a few years older than I, Kate had rough red skin and a sour disposition. She shushed me rudely every time I tried to strike up a conversation with her. Before long, I simply stopped trying.

Yes, in those years summers were difficult for me. When I wanted another child to play with, I was forced to seek out the company of Frankie Wilson, an older boy who lived in one of the neighbouring cottages. On rainy afternoons, the two of us would shoot marbles on his front porch and on sunny ones, we would play hide-and-seek in the barns and horse stalls that stood in the clearing behind his house. Frankie had a marvellous collection of tin soldiers that he would allow me to look at, but never touch. So stingy was Frankie that the only time he ever gave me permission to play with them was on the occasion of my sixth birthday. And only for a period of ten minutes. I was so envious of those tin soldiers that I begged my mother to buy me a set just like them. But Father had strong opinions about toys — he regarded them as infantile indulgences. As a result, the only childhood treats my mother could buy for me were those that could be easily concealed.

When Frankie discovered this fact, he made an effort to parade his possessions before me with even greater zeal. Frankie Wilson was a dreadful friend, but since I wasn't in a position to be choosy, I tolerated him the best I could.

The year he turned eleven, Frankie traded the tiny weapons of those tin soldiers for a real one. As hunting quickly became his new passion, the two of us stopped spending time together. Frankie died in a hunting mishap less than a year after my own passing. His death was no great loss to the world, I assure you.

My only other companion during those early years was my dear mother. With my father working long hours at the forge, Mother and I spent many of our summer days together. Away from Father's disapproving eyes, I would help her and Kate prepare the meals in the kitchen, pull weeds in the vegetable garden, talk to her of my dreams and secret ambitions as she sat and sewed in the parlour, and play cards with her for long hours into the evening while we waited for Father to return from the forge. When the weather was pleasant, we would sometimes take hikes through the forests and fields that surrounded our village. During those walks, Mother would usually pick wildflowers to fill the blue porcelain vase that rested over the hearth in the parlour. As for me, I would bring along the insect net that I had fashioned using a stick, a bit of wire, and an old pair of stockings.

You would be impressed if you could see what I was able to capture with that crude net. Even by the young age of seven, I had amassed a beautiful collection of insects, each one stuck with three pins to a smooth wooden board that was hidden under my bed. There were butterflies, caterpillars, beetles, spiders, and grasshoppers of all different colours and sizes. Under the guidance of my teacher, Mr. Brown, I hoped to collect over one hundred different specimens. So eager a student was I that Mr. Brown had promised to loan me Mr. Charles Darwin's great book, *On the Origin of Species*, the following year at school.

My mother loved to hear me speak of school and all that I was learning there. I missed my time at the schoolhouse during those summer months. Reading was one of my favourite subjects, regardless of my father's stern opinions on books. I loved borrowing novels from school and losing myself in the pages of those magical worlds. *Treasure Island, Through the Looking Glass*, and *Gulliver's Travels* were all favourites of mine and I'd spent many lunch hours reading and rereading them. Although I'd never read anything by the formidable Charles Dickens, Mr. Brown had told our class that he was one of the most important authors the world had ever known and that the entire

British Empire had been caught up with his stories. I was aching for a copy of one of his books.

My father, however, held a completely opposite opinion on the subject of learning. To my great dismay, he considered it womanish to sit around idle with a book in one's hands. As far as he was concerned, education was a dangerous waste of time. He was always grumbling about how the over-educated scientists and intellectuals of the world were ruining society with their plans and inventions. How machines would soon be replacing people and what a crime it was to steal the livelihood from honest working men. Father was determined to have me follow in his footsteps. I was destined to learn his trade and inherit his blacksmith shop. It was the duty, after all, of a family's only son to carry on where his father left off. Some called it a birthright.

As for me, I called it a curse.

The day that Father discovered my secret insect collection was beaten into my memory. I will never forget how his face erupted with a dark purple rage as he crushed all of my painstaking work under his heavy boot. When it was sufficiently ruined, he proceeded to take a switch to my backside. The following morning, before my wounds had the chance to heal, he grabbed me by the arm and pulled me up the road to where his blacksmith shop stood on Yonge Street. Then he forced me to sit immobile on a hard stool in the corner of the shop to watch him work for the rest of that day. The next morning, he hung a stained apron around my neck and set me to work fanning the bellows over the coal fire. I can only assume that Father believed that I would come to my senses if I spent enough time in his company. As if exposure to the black coal smoke would somehow ignite a love in my heart for the forge.

As you might imagine, I loathed every moment of it.

It was horribly dismal in there. By covering up all the windows with heavy curtains, the shop was kept dark so that the various colours of the hot metal could be clearly identified for work. And the constant fire from the forge combined with the summer heat outside resulted in sickeningly sweltering conditions. Because of the excessive smoke inhalation, I endured violent coughing fits all day. These became so bad that eventually my nose and eyes began to run with oily, black stuff. And with my father's constant yelling and criticism, the entire experience was eerily similar to how I envisioned hell. In my young mind, it seemed to match identically with the way our pastor described it during his weekly sermons at the Trinity Church.

Lure

Father dragged me to the forge every day for the month of July that year. I'm certain that he thought this experience was going to harden my spirit and help prepare me for my imminent destiny. But in truth, the only result was that it caused me to despise the idea of becoming a blacksmith more than ever.

The problem was that I didn't know how to tell him how much I hated his shop without incurring more of his anger. So I did the only thing I could think might save me — I confessed to my mother and begged for her help. Finally, one day in early August, Mother was able to put a stop to my torment. I happened to be listening from the stairwell as they carried on the conversation in the parlour.

"But he's so young, Robert," I heard Mother plead. Her voice always had a soft quality to it, but it had somehow become even more silken that afternoon — as soothing and melodic as a lullaby. "Let him enjoy these years without the burden of work," she continued. "There will be ample time for him to learn from you after he's grown a bit more."

"You spoil the child, Elizabeth," I heard my father growl. "Just look at him! Some physical labour will do him a world of good. It will help toughen up all the softness you've instilled in him."

"But, Robert ... you must consider his health! All

that black smoke from the fire can't be good for a young, growing body."

I heard my father snort with disgust. "Smoke bad for you? Ridiculous, woman! I breathe the smoke from the coal fire all day and I'm as strong as an ox. Since when did you become a physician, Elizabeth?"

There was a long pause during which my heart must surely have stopped. Had my mother given up the fight? Was I doomed to work in the forge for the rest of my life? My stomach began twisting into a painful nest of tight knots at the very thought. And then I heard her speak once more, her words lilting like the song of a small bird.

"Please, Robert ... just a few more years."

Tempted by curiosity, I crept forward and peeked around the corner into the parlour where my parents were engaged in their discussion. As usual, I cringed at the mere sight of my father. He was a dark, surly man, not at all like the smiling jovial fathers I've seen shepherding their children through the library in these modern times. Years of frowning and scowling had etched their marks permanently upon his face until the twin furrows between his eyebrows had grown so deep that coal dust often collected there after a long day of work. They looked like black horns rising out of his face. Of course, this only further emphasized his menacing looks as did the empty spaces between his teeth where dental rot had set in. Mother once told me that when they were married, Father had been a handsome man. As honest and forthright a woman as my dear mother was, I must confess that I found that quite impossible to believe.

Father was pacing back and forth across the room whilst lighting his pipe. I watched with trepidation as the flame from the match rose up from his hand. Then he drew in a deep breath, removed the stem from his mouth, and blew out a long stream of ghostly, grey smoke. My father's fingers were permanently blackened by the smith trade and, even now, I can vividly remember just how grimy and stained they appeared as they grasped the clean, white bowl of his pipe. While I concentrated on keeping my breaths silent so as not to give away my hiding place, Father smoked and considered his reply.

The pipe had been his wedding gift from my grandfather. It had a large, carved ivory bowl depicting a medieval hunting scene and a long, ebony stem that curved gracefully upward like the neck of a swan. Although Father never let on, I could tell how much he cherished it by the uncharacteristic tenderness he used when he carried the pipe down from the mantle. Memories of Father's pipe have stayed with me over all these years because it was the only article of any value that he kept. This was quite against his nature. Father didn't believe in owning material possessions. He likened unnecessary purchases to throwing money upon the rubbish heap. We didn't even own the house at 10 Colborne Street, choosing to rent it from a local family instead. My father was a man who was firmly set in his ways. I was painfully aware that changing his mind would not be an easy task.

"Please, Robert," Mother said again, placing her small, pale hand on his large, dirty one. I bit my lip while he took another puff from his pipe and considered her request. His black bushy side whiskers seemed to grow longer as I waited for his answer. Finally he stopped pacing, let out a rattling sigh, and gave the slightest of nods.

"Fine … a few more years, then."

I wanted to cry with relief, but fear held me back. If my father saw tears, he would surely get angry and change his mind. So instead, I crept back upstairs to continue with the painstaking task of salvaging what I could from the ruined mess of my secret insect collection. Mother had proposed the idea that my teacher, Mr. Brown, might allow me to keep it at the schoolhouse when the new term began in September.

Lure

Whether it was the threat to my health that caused Father to relent or Mother's melodic lullaby voice, I'll never know for certain. But to my knowledge, it was the first argument on the subject of my future that my mother had ever won.

And as I was to find out in the coming years, it was also to be the last.

4 — Max

I couldn't help myself. I just had to laugh. "What do you mean, a *ghost*?"

Caroline's eyes locked with mine. "Exactly what you think I mean," she replied, her voice cool as ice.

Was this girl serious? I couldn't tell by the mysterious look on her face. Her smile was frozen and her gaze steady and firm. She'd probably make an awesome poker player.

"Okay ... well, since ghosts don't exist, I figure you're talking about a Halloween prank or something?"

"No prank. I'm talking about a ghost ... spirit, phantom, spectre ... take your pick of words if you like. But it all means the same thing. This library has been haunted for years."

Man, she *was* serious. I swallowed hard, wondering what to say. This morning was getting weirder by the minute ... maybe ditching school wasn't such a good idea after all. From under the daisy patch, I could hear the sound of Peanut's high-pitched whine.

"If you don't believe me, you can ask my grandmother," Caroline added, ignoring the pug's cries. "Nana's seen and heard a lot of strange stuff since she started working here."

She was right ... I *didn't* believe her. But I wasn't going to come right out and call her crazy. I'd figured out enough about girls to know that wouldn't go over too well.

"So, what kind of strange stuff?" I asked, playing along.

Her blue eyes narrowed into slits. "You don't believe me, do you, Max?"

Perceptive, too. I'd have to watch myself around her ...

"Well, um ..." My tongue suddenly felt like it was too big for my mouth. Instead of trying to finish the sentence, I reached under the daisy patch and pulled the dog up into my arms. He stopped whining immediately, but his narrow little body was still quivering with fright.

A look of determination suddenly flashed across

Caroline's face. She reached for the library door. "Come on in and I'll take you on the ghost tour. Then we'll see if you believe."

But that just set Peanut off again. The poor little guy started barking and growling like there was a demon after him. It took all my strength to hold onto him so he wouldn't kamikaze onto the pavement.

Seeing the dog's distress, Caroline let go of the door handle and ran over to calm him down. "Okay, okay … we won't go inside," I heard her murmur into Peanut's ear. "I'm sorry, little guy." Then she looked at me and shook her head. Her golden hair swung gently from side to side. "I don't think he's going to let us go into the library today, Max. We'll have to do the tour another time. Are you going to have next Wednesday off, too?"

Next Wednesday? Was she trying to make some kind of a date with me? And then I remembered my lie from before. Something about a spare class … *oh, yeah!*

"That's right," I replied, the lie sliding across my lips like melted butter. "I don't have classes on Wednesday mornings."

"So, maybe I'll just show you the grounds today and we'll do the library next time. There haven't been any ghost sightings out here in the garden, but it's a special place. Kind of like a little piece of country right in the middle of the city."

She flashed me another smile before turning toward the garden. *Seriously, why was this girl being so nice to me?* Right up until this moment, I'd been convinced that everyone in this town was a first-class jerk.

"So, this is called a heritage garden," she said, walking ahead of me and flourishing her hand in a wide arc. Just for a quick second, she reminded me of a used-car salesman proudly displaying the contents of her lot. "It was planted to recreate what a garden would have looked like back in the 1890s. The designer used all kinds of old-fashioned seeds to make it as authentic as possible for the time period. If there was a garden on the property back then, it might have looked like this."

Then she began pointing out the different varieties of plants around us. "That's balsam over there ... and that plant is called Bridal Wreath. There's a patch of herbs behind them. And this pink coloured shrub is called Anthony Water ... um ... Water ..."

"Anthony Waterer spirea?"

Her pointing finger fell to her side as she spun around to stare at me. Her mouth was open so wide I thought a bug might fly in.

"How on earth did you know that?"

I shrugged, secretly pleased that I'd shocked her so easily. "My grandfather was a half-time gardener back in Vancouver. I used to work with him on his landscaping jobs every summer."

"A half-time gardener?" Her nose crinkled like she'd just smelled something bad. "That doesn't have anything to do with football, does it?"

I couldn't hold back a laugh. "No, it means there's not much gardening business to be done in the winter months. So from November to April, my grandfather worked as a half-time handyman. I helped him with that, too. But only on weekends."

"Wow, so you must know a lot about plants," she said, looking more relieved than impressed. I got the feeling she was just happy that I wasn't going to start talking about football.

"Yeah, and old houses, too," I added quietly. But I'm not sure if she heard that part or not.

As we made our way toward the back of the building, Caroline pointed out the last few varieties of plants. She mispronounced a couple of the names, but I didn't say anything. Instead I just listened patiently, waiting for her to get back to the topic of the ghost as she led me past a stone fountain to a small wooden bench at the edge of the grounds. We sat down on opposite ends with Peanut stretched out between us. He immediately flipped onto his back and whined for me to rub his belly. Which, of course I did. He wriggled and grunted with pleasure.

"Peanut seems to like you. Do you have a dog, too?"

I shook my head. "No, never … my mom's allergic to them."

"Huh!" She was looking at me like I was a puzzle she was trying to sort out. "So, how do you know so much about dogs, then?

"Well, my friend Lisa had one. We were, um … close."

Her left eyebrow shot up. "You and Lisa … or you and the dog?" she asked, although I sensed from her tone that she didn't really want to know the answer. So I just shut up and admired the view. Now that I saw her face up close, I realized that she was a lot younger than I'd first thought. And even prettier, too. More intrigued than ever, I fished around for more details … being careful not to sound too much like an obsessive stalker-type dude.

"So, what about you? Why aren't you in school?"

She laughed at that. "Me? I graduated last June. I'm taking the year off to work here with my grandmother, earn a bit of money, and decide what the hell

I'm going to do with my life."

Honesty ... I like that!

I cleared my throat. "So you're ... what, eighteen?"

She nodded and my heart sank.

Two years older. I don't stand a chance.

"And what about you, Max?"

"I'm ... uh, seventeen," I replied, lowering my voice just a little to make it sound more believable. It was my second lie of the morning. Well, third, if you count ditching school as a lie. *So much for honesty.* "And I just started my senior year." *Sophomore year actually. And there goes another one. Wow, they just keep rolling out of me today!*

I stopped patting the dog and started cracking my knuckles. It was a bad nervous habit, but I was desperately trying to think of a way to change the subject before she could call me out for being so dishonest. "So, are you going to tell me about the ghost now?"

"Ghost, yes ... or maybe *ghosts*," Caroline replied, her voice practically singing with secrets. "There's been so much paranormal activity in this place that some people think there might be more than one."

I tried to keep myself from laughing again. "Okay ... let's hear some stories. I'm all ears."

"Well, one of the first strange noises my nana ever

heard here was the sound of footsteps upstairs on the second level. They were light and fast, like a couple of kids running across the floor over her head. And then she heard the shutters slamming open and shut."

I shrugged, trying not to look too disappointed. *This* was her ghost story? Kind of lame. "So, maybe a couple of kids snuck up there when she wasn't looking and started fooling around?"

Caroline shook her head. "No, Nana was alone in the library at the time. And the weirdest part is that she described the footsteps as hammering and loud, like shoes knocking against hardwood. But the upstairs had just been recently carpeted so those noises didn't make sense at all. And nobody's been able to explain the shutter thing because those shutters had been bolted down for decades."

Hmm.

She leaned closer. "It's happened more than once over the years," she whispered softly; as if someone might accidently overhear us, even though we were the only ones in the garden. "I actually heard those running footsteps myself one morning back in June."

Caroline's face was only a couple of inches away from mine. Having her so close was making this awful heat ignite in the pit of my stomach ... like there was a rash spreading across my insides. Suddenly, I found myself almost wishing I could go back to being invisible again. I took a deep breath and searched for my voice. Her skin smelled like ripe peaches. *Man!* I had to fight back the sudden urge to run my fingers over her cheek.

"So, do you believe in ghosts, Max?"

"I-I-I don't know ..." I stammered, relieved to get something semi-coherent past my lips. "I guess I've never thought much about it before."

"Well, that might be about to change." Then she leaned back, taking her delicious peachy smell with her.

No ... I need more ...

She tilted her head to the side and frowned. "More what?"

Crap. Had I said that out loud?

"More ghost stories ... w-will you tell me another one?"

Dude, no wonder you haven't made any friends in this place, my humiliated brain moaned. *Would you stop acting like a lunatic?*

But thankfully, Caroline didn't seem to notice the slip.

"So you're beginning to believe, eh?" she said, flashing the gap-toothed grin again. "Sure, I'll tell you more ... next time you come around for a visit."

I must have looked disappointed because she quickly added: "Hey, it's pretty quiet around this library. I have to bring people in somehow, right? And we're open every Wednesday morning so you can feel free to come, apply for a library card, and visit as often as you want. You can fill out the forms today, if you'd like."

I could feel an angry heat start to make its way up my neck. So *that* was that it? She was just making up stories to keep people coming back to the library? Was she getting a commission for signing people up? And here I thought she genuinely wanted to see me again. Wow, I'm *such* an idiot!

She started to rise from the bench. "Now, let's go get your sub. I've got to get back to work or Nana will have my head."

I stood up faster and hoisted my backpack up onto my shoulders with such force that the books inside slammed against my ribcage. But I was too mad to notice the pain.

"Don't worry about it. I'll pick up something when I get to school. See you around."

And then I charged out of the garden before she had a chance to stop me.

5 – John

The summer of 1882 marked the first occasion of my cousin William's annual visits. For the next seven years, my cousin would arrive upon my doorstep like an uninvited pest to torment my days and nights. Looking back through the clarifying lens of time, I can see how those visits utterly defined my childhood and shaped the budding life that, tragically, never came to full fruition.

But I'm getting ahead of myself again.

The year of William's first visit I was eight years old, skinny, short-panted, and eager to please. William was ten, tall, full of potential, and brimming with resentment. Life had just dealt him a cruel blow. We'd received a letter in the spring informing us that he'd lost his father, my uncle, to typhus over the winter.

Lure

His family was preparing for rough years ahead as my Aunt Annie would be struggling to support them on her own. While she took on extra work in the summer, she'd arranged to send William to live with us for the months of July and August every year. Of course, Father grumbled about having another mouth to feed. But when Mother suggested that William would one day soon be able to help in the forge, Father relented. I secretly rejoiced at the news that I was finally to have a companion.

Lonely child that I was at the time, I was looking forward to having my cousin stay with us. I had high hopes that he would fill several voids in my life and become a playmate, a confidant, and perhaps most importantly, a distraction from my father's endless criticism.

Up until that point, the only memories I had of my cousin were from the time my family travelled to Kingston for a visit. I was five years old that summer, and William was seven. I remembered him as a fun, light-hearted fellow who enjoyed playing jacks with me in the back garden and using his mother's dinner bell to round up the neighbouring children for long afternoon games of hide-and-seek. I also remember how that visit made me yearn for a brother of my own. Now, for two months out of every year I would have something akin to a sibling.

Of course, being an only child, how could I possibly have known what the downside of that kind of relationship would be?

That afternoon, Father brought me along in the stagecoach to deliver William home from the Thornhill train station. With eager eyes, I scanned the crowds of people as they poured from the train onto the platform, looking for the boy with the toothy smile from my memories. But the young man who approached my father and extended his hand in greeting was a different person entirely. I gaped at the changes I saw in him. William had grown tall and thick in the years since our last visit and the scowl on his face betrayed the heavy state of his heart. His shoulders were hunched as if they were supporting some kind of weight. I soon discovered what it was — not difficult to figure out, for the chip on William's shoulder was a large one. As soon as we got back to Colborne Street, he began griping about being packed off to Thornhill and how the city of Kingston was superior in size and quality to our little village. I couldn't blame him for his rudeness. If I were in his shoes, I'd be resentful, too. Although only ten years of age, William was the eldest of his mother's sons. But instead of letting him take his rightful role as the new head of their household, she had treated him as a burden to be packed off and sent away. It was a humiliating blow.

My sympathy for William, however, was short-lived because, within a mere week of his arrival, he discovered an innovative way to relieve his frustrations.

By tormenting me.

As I recall, it was raining the afternoon of the first major incident. The house was ours alone as Mother was out visiting a neighbour's new baby and Father was working in the shop, finishing up an order of horseshoes for the Morgan family farm. Although the day started out in an ordinary fashion, it became memorable as the result of one impulsive decision — as all memorable days inevitably do. William had convinced me to play a game of indoor tag. When he'd first suggested it, I'd refused, of course. Tag in the house was against the rules. Although I had the sense that Mother didn't mind the playfulness of young boys, Father had strictly forbidden anything of that sort in his home.

"The barn out back is the only place for that kind of nonsense," he'd scolded whenever my young inclinations turned silly and loud. To Father, play of any kind was indulgent.

But my cousin William could be very convincing when he wanted to be.

"Nobody's here," he said, grabbing my hand and pulling me to my feet. "We can't play outside in the rain. One quick little game — come on, I'll go first. See if you can outrun me. I'll even give you a ten-second head start. One, two, three ..."

Caught up in the frenzy of his excitement, I bolted into the kitchen.

That was my first mistake.

Growling like a monster, William chased me up and down the stairs, through the parlour and around the kitchen until my heart was pounding with the thrill of the game and my head was dizzy with speed. When he finally caught up with me, he thumped me on the back, yelled "Tag!" and scrambled up the stairwell. I turned to take chase. When I reached the top of the stairs, I saw William flying across the floor of my parent's room. William's legs were longer than mine and his arms were twice as strong. No matter what game we'd played since his arrival, he always managed to beat me. And how he enjoyed lording his victories over me! But this time I was determined to win. Sensing my resolve, William ran faster than ever. He dashed to the window and pushed open the shutters with a bang. A rush of damp summer air met my face as I ran to catch him. But before I knew what was happening, he was climbing up the ledge and out on the roof of the veranda. Fast as a monkey up a tree. "Can't catch me out here!" he sang from outside. "I'm still the winner! Come on and try!"

Panting from the effort of running, I leaned my head out the window and glanced down toward the dirt road below. Vertigo seized my chest, causing me to choke on my own breath. There was no question how bad a fall I would take if my feet slipped on the smooth, wet shingles. Crushed bones would be the least of my worries.

"Oh, I see … little cousin John is afraid of heights," William taunted.

"You dirty dog!" I yelled back, anger snaking down the length of my limbs like a lit fuse. I wanted to catch him so badly that I could hardly see straight. That should have been a clear sign for me to back down. But of course, I took William's bait like the stupid fish I was back then.

It was my second mistake.

With one foot balancing on the sill and two hands clutching on to the upper part of the frame, I pulled my body out the window. I could hear my pulse throbbing in my ears as the wind whipped my hair into my eyes. Remembering it now, over a hundred years later, I can still feel that awful bitter taste rise in my mouth and the sensation that I was about to vomit from fright. But the overwhelming urge to follow William and shut him up transcended all my fears. I hesitated as the rain spat against my face. Sensing my indecision, William rose to his feet and swung his arms wildly in the air, like a turkey trying to take flight.

"Come on and catch me, chicken! Catch me now or give up the game and declare me the champion."

I lifted my other foot off the ground and was about to swing it over the window ledge when I heard the terrible growl of Father's voice from below.

"What in blazes are you two jackasses doing up there?"

I looked down and saw him standing by the front gate, hands punching his hips, and anger slashed across his face like an open wound. Petrified, I climbed down from the window with lightning speed, as if I might still have the chance to undo the damage. But, of course, it was too late. By that point, I could hear Father's steps pounding up the stairwell, coming to get me. Shutting my eyes, I cowered against the wall and waited for my punishment to come crashing down. It didn't matter that it was William's idea. It didn't matter that I hadn't followed him out onto the roof. All that mattered was that I'd disobeyed a rule and disappointed Father ... again. The price for that would be paid by my bare backside.

Lure

"William made me do it," I sobbed as he raised his arm to strike. That turned out to be the third and worst mistake of all. Through my tears, I watched as William slipped silently back inside the house to witness me take the beating of my life.

Afterward, my skin burned like someone had set it on fire. At least my cousin had the decency to bring me a glass of cool water when the beating was over. But I couldn't bring myself to thank him for it, for the look of smug satisfaction on his face had sealed up my throat with bile.

6 – Max

I wasn't planning on going back to the library. Honestly, I wasn't. But something about the place brought me there the very next Wednesday morning. Believe me when I tell you that I left my house with every intention of going to school that day. I couldn't help the fact that my feet kind of changed direction after a few minutes and started taking me toward 10 Colborne Street. It was almost like there was a giant magnet pulling me there. I'd never felt anything like it before.

Was it the house that kept me coming back?

Or the ghost stories?

Or was it Caroline?

Don't get me wrong, I was still feeling angry, and humiliated, and well ... just plain stupid about our last conversation. But I guess all of those feelings were a hundred times better than the way I felt when I was at school: *as invisible as air*. And I guess maybe after all these weeks of feeling alone, it was nice to know that someone in this crappy suburb wanted my company ... even if she *did* seem to have ulterior motives.

When I got there, I stood outside the house for a few minutes and stared up at the green shuttered windows on the second floor, remembering the story Caroline had told me the previous Wednesday. She'd sworn that those shutters were bolted down, but I knew from my experience working with Papa that fastenings came loose all the time. Especially with older buildings. A strong wind might easily have made the shutters crash open and shut in the way she'd described last week. Yeah, it was probably something as simple as that. Why was it that some people always searched for crazy theories to explain simple events?

Shaking my head, I walked up the garden path toward the side door of the library. The doubt I was feeling in the pit of my stomach was getting stronger with every step. Was I doing the right thing? Should I have come back here after what Caroline said last week? Damn! Why haven't I been able to think straight since the moment her stupid dog ran out in front of me? I'd never let a girl play around with my head like this before. Never!

I took a deep breath and stared at the tarnished door handle. One thing I did know for sure was that I'd been spending way too much time around libraries this past month. Since the start of the term, I'd passed all of my lunch hours in the school library, pretending to study even though it was too early in the year for exams or essays. Trust me, it was a better alternative to sitting alone day after day in the cafeteria like a loser. Now here I was at another library. What was wrong with me? My old friends in Vancouver would probably never recognize the kind of guy I'd become here — some kind of a bookish, girl-obsessed, social leper. Hell, I barely recognized myself.

I took a deep breath. *Okay, here goes nothing!*

My chest tightened with nerves as I pushed open the door. The rusted hinges shrieked like an old alley cat, announcing my arrival. Cringing, I let the door fall shut behind me.

Great! So much for making a subtle entrance.

I glanced around quickly to see if anybody had noticed. But the only person in sight was an old white haired lady bent over a desk. Okay, so far so good. I could still change my mind and leave if I wanted. I hesitated in the entryway for a few seconds, trying to decide what to do. My eyes jumped around, looking for Caroline, but I couldn't see her anywhere. Before I could decide if I was going to stay or not, something pushed me onward ... curiosity, stupidity, or just a case of plain old teenage hormones? Maybe all of the above.

I started walking. The floorboards creaked under my shoes with each step — my first reminder of just how old this place was. The second reminder came soon after. The smell. An overwhelming mix of musty and earthy scents hung in the air, which immediately brought back memories of my grandfather's old greenhouse in Vancouver. The one with the broken windows, dirt-covered floor, the jungle of overgrown plants, and the basket of rusted, ancient gardening tools that he would never let us replace. Papa loved gardening and had made it his mission to teach me everything he knew about plants before he passed away. That was almost a year ago, now. But I still missed him just as much as if it had happened yesterday. Shaking the sad memories off, I peered around the library, half hoping and half dreading to catch sight of *her*.

As I looked around, I was immediately struck by how much the inside of this place didn't look like a library at all. It looked like an old house. An old lady's house, to be specific. There was flower-patterned paper covering the walls, lace curtains lining the windows, plants perched on the tops of the bookshelves, and warm, rustic wooden furniture that gave it a cozy kind of feel. There was an old wooden clock in the entryway that had a fuzzy stuffed mouse running up the side. And on the opposite wall hung a series of ancient framed photos of Thornhill back from the times when Yonge Street looked like a dirt road and the most sophisticated mode of transportation seemed to be a horse and a carriage.

Were cameras really invented before cars? Guess so ...

I walked in a bit farther and came to the reception area. The old lady behind the L-shaped desk had a puffy hairdo that rose several inches off the top of her head. She was curled like the letter C over a computer keyboard, but I couldn't tell if it was because of bad work posture or one of those old-lady hunchback conditions that made her look that way. She was typing superfast and I could hear the ticking of her long nails with every stroke of the keys. I stood there waiting patiently for her to notice me.

Click-click-click ...

"Excuse me," I finally said after a long minute.

She didn't look up.

Lure

Click-click-click …

I stepped forward and dropped my backpack onto the desk with a heavy thud. Still nothing.

Click-click-click …

Either she had terrible hearing or I really was invisible!

I cleared my throat. "Um … hello," I tried again, much louder this time. It worked. The lady's eyes rose off the screen and came to rest on my face. I took a step back, trying to contain my shock as best as I could. Her thick red lipstick was bleeding into the delicate wrinkles around her mouth, making her look like a geriatric vampire.

"Oh, hello," she said with a smile that revealed a too-large-for-her-face set of perfect white dentures. "Can I help you?"

"Yeah, I'm looking for someone who works here. Her name is … "

"Max?"

I looked up to see Caroline come striding into the entryway. Surprise was radiating off her face like a beam of sunlight.

"Oh … hi. It's, uh … Wednesday," I said, unable to come up with anything better. *Stupid, stupid, stupid …*

"Yeah, I know it's Wednesday. But I didn't think you were coming back."

"Well, I um …"

The sound of a fingernail clacking against the desktop interrupted my moment of brilliance. "Speak up, please, young man. Who was it you were looking for?"

Caroline turned toward the old lady and patted her wrinkled hand, mercifully bringing the clacking to a stop. "It's all right, Nana. I think he's here to see me," she said, yelling just a bit.

Oh crap! This was her nana? How was that even possible? She looked like she had to be at least a hundred years old.

I leaned in for a closer look — yeah, I guess I could sort of see it. The old lady's eyes were the exact same sky-blue colour as Caroline's. But that really seemed to be where any family resemblance ended. I forced out my most polite, grandmother-pleasing smile. "Thanks for your help, ma'am."

Her watery eyes scanned my face for a couple more seconds before dropping back down to the computer screen. "Crazy kids," she muttered.

Click-click-click …

And just like that, I was invisible again. I sighed, suddenly wishing I hadn't come this morning. Maybe this was a mistake. Maybe I should just leave and …

A floor board creaked loudly to my left. I turned to see Caroline standing beside me, staring up into my face. Her gap-tooth smile was back. My stomach felt like it was being hit with a hammer.

"I'm glad you're here, Max," she said. "I was hoping you'd come this morning."

"Yeah ... I, well ... me, too." *Idiot, idiot, idiot!*

"So, can I give you that tour now?"

This time I just shut my mouth and nodded to avoid further embarrassment. Caroline stepped forward and motioned toward the room on the right.

"Great. We can start with the parlour."

Like a moron, I just nodded again. Sweeping past, Caroline led me into a large square room lined with bookcases.

"So, back when this was a house, this was the room where families would have received their guests and spent their social time. Playing cards, drinking tea, that kind of thing. And if they'd had a piano, it would have been here."

My eyes did a 360-sweep of the room. In the middle were a couple of small couches, some chairs, and a coffee table with local newspapers and magazines laid out in three straight lines. The inside of the red front door stood against the far wall flanked by candle holders on either side. More old-lady quaintness. It was quite possibly the most normal-looking room I'd ever seen in my life.

"Okay ... and this is where your friend's dog went crazy, right? Because he saw a ghost?" It was the longest sentence I'd managed since I'd walked through the door and somehow, I was able to untie my tongue and get the words out without tripping all over them.

Caroline turned to examine my face, like she was trying to figure out if I was serious about the ghost thing or not. Hoping to look convincing, I beat back the cynical smirk that was struggling to come out and betray me.

"Yeah, that's right," she said after a moment. "It was here in this room. And the dog hasn't stepped a paw into the parlour ever since. It must have seen some wickedly evil spirit."

Trying to force a serious look into my eyes, I nodded like I believed her. "And I think you were going to tell me some *new* stories about the ghost this time, remember?"

"Yes, that's right ... I did say that, didn't I?" She pointed to one of the windows. "Well, recently we've smelt a strong scent of cologne in the parlour right over in that part of the room ... but like, first thing in the morning when there's been nobody in the library. It's very strange."

I took another look around the room, trying to see if I sensed anything unusual about the place. I took a deep breath through my nose, but I couldn't smell anything except for that musty damp odour that was everywhere. And there was no sound except for the ticking of the clock in the entryway. Really, it was just a room full of books and DVDs ... nothing more. But I didn't want to disappoint Caroline, so I stayed quiet.

"Okay, let's move on," Caroline said, stepping out of the parlour. Her hair bounced on her shoulders with every creaky step. I followed close behind, hoping to catch a hint of that peachy smell again.

"So, speaking of dogs, how's Peanut doing?" I asked, enjoying how steady and cool my voice was sounding. This wasn't so hard, after all. For a minute there, I was starting to feel like the old me again.

And then Caroline laughed and tossed her hair back over her shoulder. "He's at home today. Probably curled up in my bed right now, the little devil."

Her bed? The mental image of her sleeping in it with her blonde hair fanned out across the pillow brought the hammer pounding back into my stomach again. Damn! There went my chill. But, thankfully, she didn't seem to notice because she kept walking. A few more paces and we stopped in front of a narrow stairwell just to the left of the reception desk. There was a bunch of different warning signs hanging above.

Staff only beyond this point ... Caution low clearance ... Notice: Authorized Personnel Only.

"Are you guys keeping government secrets up there, or what?" I said with a laugh, pointing at the collection of signs.

Out of the corner of my eye, I saw Nana glance up from her typing. But the clacking of her nails never once slowed down. Was she writing her life story on that thing, or what?

"This is the original stairwell to the second floor," Caroline explained. "A few years ago, one of the librarians was unloading a trolley of books right here where we're standing. She looked up to see a pair of high-buttoned boots and the bottom of a grey calico skirt on the landing. She tried to scream, but her voice was missing ... like it had been grabbed from her throat."

I swallowed back a lump that was rising in my own throat as my brain reached for an explanation. "And so? What happened next?"

"A co-worker passed by and asked her what she was staring at. And why her face was so pale and frightened. But when she tried to point out the boots and explain what she'd seen, they were gone. The stairwell was empty again ... just like how it looks now."

Lure

I stared up again into the narrow passage. There was nothing there but a tower of stairs covered with worn, grey carpet.

"And there's more," Caroline said. "If you're interested, that is."

"That's why I'm here, right?" I replied, hoping she was still buying the act ... that I didn't come back just because I wanted to see her again.

"Okay, well there have been a lot of reports about people smelling smoke in the house. Like there's something burning. But not an unpleasant kind of smoke ... more like something from a pipe or a cigar. And the smell seems to be especially strong right here in the stairwell."

"Have you smelled it?"

"No, but Nana has. And so have a few other librarians. I don't know what it means, or how it's related to the ghosts. Whenever it happens, it always causes a lot of alarm because they're worried there could be a fire somewhere. But every time people go searching for the source of the smoke they can't seem to find anything."

I leaned forward and took a deep breath. I was just expecting to inhale more of my grandfather's greenhouse memories. But there it was — the unmistakeable fragrance of burning tobacco filling my nose.

And it wasn't an old, lingering odour ... it was as fresh and sharp as if someone was smoking right there beside me. My heart began to beat a bit faster. I turned back to look at Caroline. *Could she smell that, too? Did I even want to ask? What the hell did it mean? Was there a ghost here now?* Suddenly I heard a whisper of a sound ... like a long, deep breath blowing through the stairwell. A shiver crept over my skin, but I shook it off, forcing myself to remember how ridiculous this whole thing was. I didn't believe in ghosts.

"So, let's have a look up there," I said, pointing up the stairway. It's not as if I actually expected to see the ghost sitting on the top step waiting for me, dragging on a cigarette. Caroline glanced around to see if anyone else was watching. Nana appeared to still be absorbed with her computer. We were safe. "Um, okay ... quickly, though. It's supposed to be just for library staff, but I'll show you if we go fast."

With a nod, I took a step forward and conked my forehead against the overhang of the stairwell.

Ow! Damn it!

I recoiled backwards, as if I'd been punched. Caroline was instantly at my side, peering through my mop of brown hair to find the injury. Her hands fluttered nervously around my head like a pair of butterflies. The smell of ripe peaches filled my nose, overtaking any lingering scent of tobacco. The room shifted slightly to the left.

"Oh God, I'm sorry, I should have warned you about the low overhang. I guess you're, um, pretty tall." Her eyes dropped down to the floor.

Holy crap, was she blushing?

"Yeah, I guess I am," I replied, struggling to keep a respectable amount of cool in my voice while my head throbbed with pain.

"I don't think people got to be as big as you back in those days," she continued after a moment. "You know ... what with malnutrition and diseases and all those things. So doorways and ceilings were lower. And stairwell overhangs, too ..." Suddenly, her fingers stopped fluttering and she lowered her hands back to her sides. "Okay, I saw it — it's just a small, red mark, no blood or anything." But I could tell that she was still worried. Her blue eyes searched my face for signs of trauma. They were practically glowing in the dim light of the stairwell. "So, are you all right?"

I think I nodded.

She sighed and her shoulders sank with relief.

"Could you maybe just try to duck a bit so we won't have to take you to the emergency room?"

And then she smiled. The gap reappeared, taunting me like a glimpse of a secret passageway to another world. All I could do was nod stupidly.

Just like the idiotic, girl-obsessed social leper I'd clearly become.

7 — John

In the summer of 1885, I was eleven and William was thirteen. My cousin was still coming to stay with us every summer and that heavy chip on his shoulder was still firmly in place. But, naive as I was back then, I wasn't able to understand that doing harm to me was the only way William thought he'd be able to knock the chip loose.

"Hello, John," he'd said simply as I greeted him at the train station. Father had sent me in alone to fetch him while he waited in the stagecoach outside. "Are you really old enough to be here by yourself?"

William's voice was almost unrecognizable and the mere sound of it caused me to take a small step back. It had deepened in the past year. And there was a faint shadow of a beard hiding under the skin on his chin. For a split second, I was afraid of him. But, of course, I didn't let on. I knew to do so would invite a level of mischief and taunting that I'd surely never before had to endure.

"Father's outside in the carriage," was all I could manage to say in reply.

The visit started out smoother than any previous year. I thought perhaps William had matured over the winter because he seemed to be on his best behaviour. Until, that is, one day in mid-July.

It was my parent's twentieth wedding anniversary. Mother surprised all of us by presenting Father with a bottle of French cologne for the occasion. Of course, Father complained bitterly about how ridiculous it was and how men shouldn't act like women and put on airs, and how the smell of a good, honest, hard-working blacksmith was surely better than any foolish high-priced bottled water from France. But in the end, he agreed to put it on just as I knew he would. Mother almost always got her way with him (when the matter didn't involve me, of course). I could smell the musky cologne lingering in the parlour air for a while after they'd left for lunch at the Yonge Street Hotel.

Of course, William tried to convince me to put on some of the cologne myself before we left for our fishing trip over at the nearby Don River. "Don't you know? Cologne helps keep the mosquitoes away."

But in the three years since William had started visiting, I'd finally learned not to fall into his traps. I wasn't a gullible child anymore.

Or so I liked to think.

That was the first indication that William's good behaviour had come to an end. The second came later that night when he first stole the pipe. I was sleeping at the time.

"Look what I've got," hissed a voice beside my head.

I opened my eyes to the sight of William shaking me awake. I stared through the blackened room until my eyes adjusted and I could see his face. I knew by the depth of the darkness that it must be the middle of the night ... what did he want now?

"What is it?" I mumbled, my mouth full of feathers.

"Look ... let's have a smoke."

He thrust an object into my face. It took me a few seconds to recognize that it was my father's pipe. The carved ivory bowl glowed like a ghost in the darkened room. White bone emerging from wet, black soil.

"We can't smoke that," I gasped. "Father will whip us if he finds out we took his pipe."

"Come, he'll never find out. We'll do it away from the bedrooms. And I'll put it back on the mantle as soon as we're done."

Somehow, through the darkness, he must have sensed my fears. Like it was a smell seeping out of my pores.

"Don't worry, the pipe will have cooled completely by morning. There will be not a trace left of our transgression. I promise."

Transgression. That word had always possessed a strange power to make me feel guilty — the sound of it was like a priest breathing down my neck. I rolled over and pulled the quilt up over my ear.

"Leave me alone, William," I begged.

For a brief moment, there was blissful silence and I truly thought he was going to go away and leave me be. My eyes closed with relief. But an instant later, William was yanking the quilt from my shoulders and spitting venom into my face. His voice was a cruelly pinched falsetto:

"Little John, always so afraid. You should have your mother sew you a dress and a bonnet because you'd get on much better in this life as a girl."

My stomach twisted into a hard knot. When had William begun to sound just like Father? An owl hooted somewhere outside my window. *Hoo-hoo-who will prevail?* My eyelids drooped with exhaustion. Dear God, all I wanted was to roll over and go back to sleep. But my pride was at stake. Damned pride!

"Yes, fine. I'll smoke the pipe with you."

Tossing off my quilt, I got out of bed and followed William out of the room. My bare feet slapped against the cold wooden floor like fishtails against the surface of water. It was a cool night. More than anything, I wanted to run back to my bedroom and put on a pair of stockings but I feared that would invite more taunting from William, so I just kept going.

"We should do it in the stairwell," he whispered over his shoulder.

I stopped in my tracks. "The stairwell? But why? If my parents wake up, we'll be caught!"

"Trust me," William hissed, grabbing me by the arm and pulling me along. "It's the perfect place. There's a draft in the stairwell that will carry the smell away from the bedrooms. And if we hear them coming, we can run downstairs and replace the pipe before your father can find it missing."

This whole thing was giving me a stomach ache. But, of course, William didn't care about that. He sat down on the top step and produced a box of matches from behind his back. My eyes bulged with surprise. Apparently, he'd stolen more than just

Father's pipe. William lit the tobacco and sucked on the stem until a wisp of smoke began to curl out of the bowl, like a snake rising out of the charmer's basket. Then he passed it to me and waited for me to take my turn. I hesitated.

"Go on, John," William hissed. "We don't have all night."

Closing my eyes, I took a small drag on the pipe. Right from the first puff, I felt like my lungs were collapsing. Muffling a cough in my hand, I passed it back to my cousin, silently hoping that now I could return to my bed. But William wouldn't let me leave until we'd smoked every bit of tobacco in that pipe. "You'll enjoy it when you have more practice," he kept promising. He was wrong. The whole experience was just awful.

Our nighttime smoking sessions became a regular habit that summer. Each one of them followed an identical pattern. William would wake me up with Father's pipe in his hand and taunt me until I agreed to come with him to the stairwell. The smoke would bring on coughing fits every time, which we would be forced to smother with our hands. It was terrible. And yet, night after night we continued to do it.

At first, I couldn't understand why my cousin wanted to smoke that pipe so desperately. But after a few weeks I began to understand. And by the time we were finally discovered, I had developed a taste for the tobacco and was enjoying the smooth feeling of the smoke inside my throat. Holding the pipe felt forbidden, dangerous, grown-up. It certainly made me feel like more of a man than working in the forge ever had. But that meant nothing to Father who, as you might imagine, gave me the beating of my life when he came upon me one night with his stolen pipe in my hand. When he was done, my skin was so raw that I couldn't walk for two days. But my pride hurt worse than anything I'd ever experienced. I had let myself be duped by my cousin yet again.

I vowed to myself that it would be the last time.

8 – Max

Ducking low this time around, I followed Caroline up the stairwell to the second floor of the house. There wasn't much to see up there ... just a big room with a long table and some chairs. And there were two little rooms that opened up off to the side.

"These were the bedrooms, I guess?"

"Yup," she replied, leading me into a tiny room facing the street.

"Wow, it's small," I said, turning around slowly. There was barely enough room to put a bed. *And I thought my room in our new house was cramped!*

"Remember what I just told you ... people weren't as big back then. And most of the families in those days were pretty large, so the children would have had to share these rooms with their siblings."

I glanced around. "And where was the bathroom?"

She giggled at that. "There was no indoor plumbing back in those days, Max. They had to use an outhouse … or a chamber pot if it was a cold night."

Chamber pots? I could not even imagine having to take a leak in a bucket in my own bedroom. Thank God I was born after toilets were invented!

She pointed to the other little room. "The reason I brought you up here was to show you this bedroom. There was another apparition seen in here. A man returning a book to the outdoor drop box late one night claimed to have seen the greyish silhouette of a woman standing right there at that window."

I walked over to the tiny window and looked out to the street below. "And do you think it was the same ghost who was wearing the high-buttoned boots on the stairwell?"

She shrugged. "I have no idea. All we know is that each time there's been an apparition, it's been a woman."

I turned away from the window. Caroline was standing in the narrow doorway, chewing on her pinky fingernail. For a second there, she looked just like a nervous little kid.

"Do you have any idea who the woman is … well, I mean, *was*?"

She shook her head. "Some people think it's the ghost of Ellen Ramsden, the first owner of this house. But this building changed hands many times over those years, so it really could be any one of the old inhabitants. Or even someone else who might have had connections to this place."

I stepped toward her, the ancient floorboards groaning beneath my running shoe. "Hey, you know maybe you should think about studying history when you go to university," I said. "You're pretty good at remembering all these old facts about dead people."

Her eyes dimmed ... like a light inside her head had just been switched off. "Guess you could say I'm a bit of an expert in that department," she mumbled. Then she turned and walked back to the stairwell. "I think we should get back downstairs now ... I'm not really supposed to let people up here."

There wasn't much else to see in the bedrooms so I was glad to go back downstairs. At that point, I thought the tour was over, but it turned out that Caroline still had one room left to show me. To the left of the stairs was another large room full of bookshelves.

"This is the Fiction room. It was also part of the original house ... most likely the kitchen. The rest of the library beyond this point was added on in later years."

Lure

I looked around. There was nothing to see in this room except for books.

"Okay ... so, is that it for the ghost tour?" I asked. Was this the part when she collects her commission and makes me sign up for that library card? I waited for the sales pitch. But it didn't come. Instead, she just grinned and bobbed up and down on her toes. The light in her eyes was back again.

"No, not at all. I've saved the best for last," she said, waving her hand in the direction of a narrow, sunlit window crammed in a space between the bookshelves. "The most famous apparition of all was of an old woman sitting in a rocking chair right there in that spot. She was covered in light, rocking back and forth and repeating the name *John, John, John,* over and over again. That was a long time ago but a couple of the other librarians have heard moaning coming from that exact spot over the years."

An army of goosebumps began a slow march up my arms toward my neck.

"All right ... so who was John?"

Caroline turned back to look at me, her blue eyes like ice. "I wish I could tell you, Max."

"Well, can't they look through the old records? There should be a way to see if someone named John lived here when it used to be a house?"

What I wanted to say was that this was finally a chance to get some real evidence to hold up all her crazy ghost stories. But, of course, I didn't.

Caroline crossed her arms in front of her chest and smirked in a self-satisfied kind of way. "So, does this mean that you're finally admitting that you believe in ghosts?"

"No ... not at all," I replied, suddenly defensive. "It's just that some proof would make these stories a lot more believable."

"Well, we did look through the old records and there were a lot of Johns who lived here. Remember, it was a very popular name back then. Ellen Ramsden was married to a John. And her son was named John, too. And the owner who came after her was named John. And so was his son. And there's a big gap in the record-keeping between 1860 and 1890."

"A gap? Why?"

"The building was rented out between those years. So, I guess there's a chance that John was someone who lived here during that time. But, of course, all of this is based on the assumption that you believe in ghosts."

I didn't believe in ghosts, did I? I honestly didn't know what I thought anymore. This girl was seriously playing with my head. Suddenly, I heard the faint sound of a door slamming from upstairs. My head whipped around. There was Nana still sitting and typing at the reception desk where she'd been all along.

"Did you hear that noise?" I whispered, turning back to Caroline.

She shook her head. "Are you okay, Max? You look pale."

Grabbing my backpack, I stumbled out of the room. "I ... I have to go now. I've got some studying to do before my afternoon classes."

Although I didn't turn around to see her face, I could tell from the little whine in her voice that Caroline was sorry to see me leave. "Okay. But will you come visit me again next week? I'll try to remember some new ghost stories for you ..."

"Yeah ... no ... I'll see you later," I said, hurrying through the entryway. No promises. I wanted to walk out the door and breathe fresh air again. I wanted to race down the garden path and never come back. I wanted to forget everything about this place. But I knew that would be impossible. I would be back ... and it would be soon. The lure was too strong.

Yanking down the handle, I hurled open the door and charged outside into the crisp autumn morning. My body heaved with relief as I gulped down the fresh air. I felt like a drowning man who'd just been pulled from the water in the nick of time.

9 – John

During the summer of 1886, I received some terrible news; news that I had been dreading since I was old enough to read. Father had made the final decision about my future. My mother relayed the tragic details to me on the morning of my twelfth birthday while the two of us were in the parlour preparing to leave for church. Her usual gentle countenance was clenched with regret.

"John, I'm very sorry," she said, her voice reduced to a dry whisper, "but your father has decided that the time has come …"

The mantle clock ticked loudly behind us as Mother's voice faded to silence. But certainly she had no need to explain further. I understood immediately to what she was referring and the words felt like knives cleaving my heart.

Simply stated, I was doomed. My father wanted me to start work in the forge. My life as a student was over. I felt like a prisoner who had just been condemned to a life sentence of hard labour.

"But Mother, I'm only just turning twelve," I said, careful to keep my voice low so Father wouldn't overhear me. "I had thought my apprenticeship could wait until I was fourteen."

Her fingers twisted and writhed in her lap while her eyes begged for understanding. "John, please ..." was all she could say. I jumped up from the settee and began pacing back and forth across the floor, each step in time with the hammer of my heart.

"Can't you speak to him about this?" I begged, my voice rising with desperation. "Can't you make him change his mind?"

My mother's head wobbled slightly, as if her neck were suddenly too weak to support its weight. "I can try speaking to him again, John. But, as you know, your cousin William is to begin his apprenticeship this year and your father believes that it would be easier to teach both of you at the same time. I must confess — it doesn't help matters that your father's mood seems to be unusually sour today. He will be difficult to persuade."

I hung my head to hide the spasm of pain that was gripping my face. Every year on my birthday, Father's mood grew darker than his coal-stained fingernails. I can only surmise that it was because the day reminded him of how unlucky he was. The day the Lord above had chosen to curse him with a weak son.

The floorboards creaked beneath my shoes as I increased my pace. Rising from the settee, Mother followed behind me as I marched across the floor, still wringing her hands with guilt. I could hear the swish of the crinoline underneath her calico skirt as she struggled to keep up with my steps. At that age, I wasn't yet old enough to be embarrassed by the thought of a woman's skirts. As it turned out, I never would be.

"Please speak with him, Mother. I would sooner run away from home than give up my studies to work in the forge," I said, my voice trembling with anger.

"I'll do my best, John. But you know how your father feels about school."

"I don't understand! What's wrong with him that he cannot see the value in book-learning?" I asked, my voice rising with the heat of my anger. "Why can't I stay on and study to become a teacher, like Mr. Brown?"

My teacher was the smartest man I'd ever met. While most people needed their slate to figure out numbers, Mr. Brown could do any math equation in his head in a matter of seconds. Some of the older students and I would often stay inside at lunchtime to test him. Mr. Brown hasn't gotten one math problem wrong yet. I don't think he ever will! And he's read over three hundred books in his life, which means he's probably read every book that has ever been written (for back then, I couldn't imagine more than three hundred books in the world). My secret dream was to read just as many books myself — although it would have to be in secret. At least until the day I moved out of my father's house.

Naturally, at the time I had no way of knowing that day would never arrive.

My mother reached out and touched my shoulder. So tiny a woman was she; the weight of her hand was no heavier than a grasshopper upon my skin. By the age of twelve I'd already surpassed her height. And I was by no means a large child.

"Hush, my love," she warned, "... he's just upstairs. What if he hears you?"

We both knew how it would enrage Father to know about my secret ambitions. If I'd been born a girl, becoming a teacher wouldn't have been a problem. But Robert McCallum considered books to be idle and womanish, and male teachers effeminate and weak. There was no chance that he would sanction a career in book-learning for me. No, he would do whatever he had to do to ensure that his only son learned his trade and took over the forge. A hammer, an anvil, and a coal fire were the tools of my future. Books were not.

Dear God in heaven, I suddenly hated him with so much force that I could barely form a complete thought. My eyes came to rest on Father's pipe, sitting in its usual place on the mantle. It took every ounce of my willpower to keep myself from hurling it to the floor and stomping it to dust under my shoe. Frustrated, I stopped pacing for a moment and tried one more time.

"What if Father would let me stay at school for just another two years? Then I'll come to work with him. I'll give him my solemn promise."

Mother's face swelled with a combination of love and pity as she looked upon my face. I often wondered if my mother saw the souls of all her eleven children staring back at her from my eyes. For it was as if she drew all the love for the lost ones together into a deep, concentrated adoration of me.

The sudden thump of Father's footsteps on the stairwell caused both of us to jump with fright.

"I'll do my best, John," she whispered, her hands

rushing to smooth out the folds of her skirt as the heavy stomp of his boots drew nearer.

But unfortunately, as I was to learn later that night, my father was adamant about his decision.

Whilst preparing for bed, I discovered a birthday present hidden under my pillow. It was a book. A beautiful hardback copy of *David Copperfield* by Charles Dickens. The first book I'd ever owned. The first book on my way to three hundred. After I'd caught my breath back, I opened the cover carefully and inhaled the inky smell of the fresh new pages. A folded piece of creamy notepaper fell out and landed on my lap. Still clutching the book, I unfolded the note and read:

Happy Birthday to my beloved son.

I am so very sorry, but your father will not be persuaded. I promise to do what I can to make the situation bearable for you. Your collection of books has begun today. Be sure to keep this in a safe place and please let it be our little secret.

As always,
Your loving Mother

Deborah Kerbel

For the remainder of my short life, I received a secret book from my mother on my birthday every year. It was the only way she knew how to apologize for failing me.

10 – Max

Caroline was sitting cross-legged in the middle of a dirty, dusty floor. She was holding a small, white cat in her lap and looking up at me with eyes that were wide with fear.

"No, don't kill him, Max!" she cried. Her lips weren't moving with the words, but I could hear her voice breaking somewhere in her throat. I stared at her in shock.

Kill who? The cat? Why would I do that?

When I started walking toward her, she clutched the little animal to her chest and began to scream, although her mouth still wasn't moving. I wanted to run and comfort her, but I was frozen in place by her fear. *What's going on here?* My thoughts were spinning with the force of so much confusion that I thought I was going to fall over. I tried to widen my stance to regain some balance, but I couldn't force my feet to move even an inch. That's when I looked down and saw a long hunting knife in my hand, the blade glistening like water. I opened my own mouth to scream, but nothing came out. I tried harder, horrified by the monster I'd clearly become. But it was like I was choking on the air. I couldn't catch a breath. Finally, I managed to suck in a small bubble of oxygen and push out a low, guttural yell.

"Aaaaaaaaaah!"

The effort of making the sound is what raised me up out of the dream. Or nightmare, to be exact. I opened my eyes, gasping for air, and blinking through the darkness, the leftover yell still buzzing in my throat.

Just a dream, I told myself, sitting up in bed. But my pounding heart needed a bit more convincing. It wasn't until I switched on my bedside lamp that I realized my sheets were soaked with water. And the skin on my arms and chest was shining with sweat. But was it sweat? I wasn't hot at all. In fact, I was shivering from the cold night breeze that was blowing in through my window.

What's going on? I don't remember going to sleep with it open.

Lure

But the weirdest part of all was the smell that was coming off my wet skin. It was dank and raw and earthy ... like a mix of worms and frogs. I smelled more like an old swamp than a sweaty guy. In fact, the stink was so overpowering I disgusted myself. Throwing off the covers, I stumbled out of my room and into the shower. I needed to wash the smell away and hopefully the memory of the nightmare would go down the drain along with it.

By the time I was clean and dried off, it was too late to go back to sleep. But it was too early to go to school. So I grabbed a piece of toast and my backpack and went for a walk. I needed to clear my head and getting outside into the fresh autumn air was the best way to do that. Walking up and down the early morning streets offered me a view of this town I hadn't seen before. I watched the bright orange sun peek over the rooftops as it climbed in the sky to start the new day. I watched the houses wake up, bathrobed men and women collect their newspapers, dogs sniff around on their morning walks, frantic adults rush into their cars, and bouncy children jump through the leaves as they headed off to school. I walked and walked and walked some more, trying as hard as I could to keep my feet away from 10 Colborne Street.

It was Wednesday again. I didn't want to go back there today, especially since I'd caught hell from my parents for ditching the past couple of Wednesday-morning classes. But after last night's dream I was aching to see Caroline and make sure she was all right. And could I even stay away if I tried? She's the only one who could really see me around here. But the agonizing part was that she only saw me as a friend. I still didn't know if I could handle that.

Giving in, I finally let my feet guide me back to the little white house on Colborne Street. It was almost as if there were a pair of hands pushing me to go faster as I marched up the driveway toward the garden path. The library wasn't open yet; it was still too early. I glanced down at my watch and took a seat on the bench at the back of the garden to wait for her. After a couple of minutes, a small, brown rabbit hopped across the path, nose twitching as it searched for some breakfast. It quickly discovered a small patch of clover beside the picket fence and stopped to munch for a while. My stomach growled as I watched the rabbit eat, wishing I'd grabbed more than a thin slice of toast from home. I thought about running over to Yonge Street and picking up a cup of coffee, but I wanted to catch Caroline before she went into the library. So I just stayed put and ignored the grumbles from my gut.

Lure

About twenty minutes later she came strolling up the path, wearing the exact same sweater she'd been wearing in my dream last night. That freaked me out more than a little bit, but I tried not to let it show on my face. When she spotted me sitting at the back of the garden she stopped in shock, keys frozen in her outstretched hand.

"Max! God, you scared me. What are you doing here? We're not even open yet."

"I … I was up early this morning," I said, getting to my feet. I couldn't explain it, but suddenly I had an overwhelming need to get her away from this place and all its history and ghosts … and grandmothers. "Hey, do you need to get right to work? I thought we could go for a walk or something?"

She pulled up her sleeve to check her watch. "Well, I guess I can go for a little bit. Nana will probably be here soon and she can open up the library today."

I flung my backpack over my shoulder and strode toward her. "Great … let's go."

Together, we walked up the tree-lined road away from the screeching river of traffic coursing up and down Yonge Street. I was being careful to keep a safe, wide bubble of space between the two of us, nervous about the moronic things I might say or do if we got too close.

"So, do you feel any closer to making your decision?" I asked, hoping to get the conversation going. I usually didn't mind sharing a good silence with a friend, but with Caroline it felt better having something to say. I knew the words were going to help me maintain that bubble.

She turned to look at me, confusion creasing her pretty face. "What decision?"

"You know ... the decision about what the hell you want to do with your life next year?"

I thought that would prompt a smile, but she frowned instead. "Oh, yeah ... that."

And then silence. I rushed in to fill it ... maybe a little too fast.

"You know, my mom keeps telling me about all the great schools they have out here on this side of the country. Not that we don't have great schools out west, but I guess there's more of them over here. So, have you been looking into any of the programs?"

"Um ... no, not really. I don't think I'm ready to start thinking about university yet," she replied, her voice far away. That's when I noticed her fingers. They were twisting and pulling the sleeves of her sweater into tight little knots. Suddenly, I had the sinking feeling that I'd said something wrong. If only I knew what. Man, why was this girl so freaking mysterious?

Lure

This time when the silence came back, I left it alone to do its thing. Seconds stretched out between us. At least the sound of our shoes crunching through the carpet of dried leaves made it a bit less unbearable.

"Hey, have you ever noticed some of the other historic homes on this street, Max?" she asked after a long moment, pointing to the sagging red house on our left. "Here's one that's even older than the library."

Yeah, she was definitely trying to change the subject.

"Um … no, I guess not," I replied, going along with it. I was just happy to have something safe to talk about. Following the direction of her finger, I saw that this house had a plaque, too. It read: *William Lane; cooper, 1846.*

"There are lots of them along here," she continued, a trace of pride rounding out her words. "Nana once told me that Colborne is probably the best-preserved historic street in all of Ontario. Look, there's another one right there."

I looked over to see a plump, motherly looking woman raking a pile of yellow leaves in her driveway. She glanced up from her rake and smiled as we passed her house. My eyes skipped up to search for the plaque … yup, there it was to the right of the front door. *Job Trott; mason, 1851.*

"I don't get it," I said, shaking my head. "Regular people are allowed to live in these houses? I thought they were historic buildings."

Caroline nodded. "They are ... but they're also homes. Of course, the owners have to conserve the outside of the buildings as best as they can. But they were built to be lived in."

Honestly, this had to be the most surreal street I'd ever seen. It was almost like I'd left the real world and been transported to the film set of a historical movie. I spotted another old house on the opposite side of the road and went to take a closer look. *Thomas Hamill; carpenter, 1850.* Too bad my parents hadn't known about this street when they were house-hunting in Thornhill. It might have been cool to live in one of these old cottages. I wanted to ask Caroline if any of them were haunted like the library. But I decided to ask a different question instead.

"So, are you all out of ghost stories ... or are there any more you've been holding back?"

She nibbled on her lower lip while she thought about the question. My eyes dropped so I wouldn't have to watch. I studied the frayed ends of my shoelaces while I waited for my pulse to slow back down. After a moment, she came up with an answer.

Lure

"Once or twice I thought I heard the sound of books being pulled off the shelves and the pages flipping. It happened when I was there alone in the morning. And sometimes Nana or I will be searching for a particular book for hours and we'll decide that it's gone missing ... then there it is on the shelf the very next day, right where it should have been all along."

This time it was totally impossible to keep the skepticism out of my voice. "That doesn't make any sense, Caroline — if they were really ghosts, how on earth could they move the books?"

The familiar Mona Lisa smile tugged at her lips. "Do some research into it, Max. You'll see that ghosts can have a physical presence if they want to."

I was about to change the subject when something weird suddenly occurred to me. "Okay, so you've smelled and heard strange things in the library ... but you've never actually *seen* anything yourself?"

"Well, no."

I shook my head and sighed. "I just don't get it. If you haven't seen anything, then how can you believe so strongly in the ghost?"

To my surprise, Caroline just laughed at that. "I guess there're lots of things I've never seen that I still believe in."

"Like what? Santa Claus?" I asked, slightly irritated. I didn't enjoy being such a constant source of amusement to her.

She looked at me and flashed her gap-toothed smile. "Well, I've never seen *love*. But I still believe in it."

Suddenly, I didn't want that safe bubble of space between us anymore. In fact, I wanted to take her hand so badly my fingers were itching with desperation. But I didn't. I kept them tucked away inside my jean pockets instead. I had already embarrassed myself enough around this girl without making a move like that. She was smart, sweet, beautiful ... and two years older. I knew that there was no way in hell she would ever be interested in a kid like me.

We walked in silence for a full minute before she spoke again.

"I've never told anyone this, Max," she said, her voice barely louder than a whisper, "I haven't even told Nana. But I really want to tell you. I did see something happen ... just once. It was back in the middle of September, a few days before you and I met."

"Okay, what was it?" I asked. We'd just turned a corner and were walking south along a narrow road.

"It only happened once, when I was there on my own. It was late in the evening and I was cleaning up, getting ready to close the library. I looked up at the clock … you know the one in the entryway with the toy mouse climbing up the front?"

I nodded. "Yeah, I know it."

"Well, I was checking to see if it was time to turn the sign in the window from 'open' to 'closed.' That's when I saw …"

I stopped walking and waited for her to finish. "Saw what?"

She stopped, too. I watched her shoulders rise as she took a slow, deep breath. "The second hand was turning the wrong way. You know … like, backwards. And then the hour and minute hands started to turn and spin backwards, too."

Now *this* was getting interesting. "Okay … and then what happened?"

Her blue eyes met mine. "I didn't wait around to find out. I was so scared, I closed up and ran out of there."

"And so nobody else saw this? You don't have a witness?"

She shrugged and started walking again. "Nope. Sorry, no proof on this one, either."

I raked my fingers back and forth through my hair, trying to come up with a rational explanation for this. I knew for sure there was *always* a rational explanation if you looked hard enough.

Wasn't there?

"Well, couldn't it just have been a battery malfunction? Or something faulty with the gears of the clock?"

She tilted her steps slightly away, widening the space between us. "Look, I guess it could have been but I highly doubt it," her words were sharp, like I'd touched on a raw nerve. "I have a feeling that it means something important. Like whoever is haunting the library is wishing they could turn back time — you know, go back and fix something they didn't have a chance to when they were alive. Right a wrong from the past ..."

This was all a bit too much for me. I don't think I'd ever heard such a far-fetched theory in my life. "You actually think ghosts have regrets?"

"Yeah, I definitely do."

I was about to reply when suddenly Caroline stopped walking and pointed to the left. "Okay, so we're here. Want to go in for a little bit?"

I hadn't been watching where we were going since we'd left the library. So I was shocked to find myself standing at the entrance to a graveyard. A bronze sign facing the road read: *Thornhill Cemetery*. Without waiting for my reply, Caroline walked straight in through the black iron gates, like there was nothing unusual about the place at all. When she realized that

I wasn't keeping up, she stopped and spun around to face me.

"Hey, aren't you coming?" she asked, waving me over.

I was still standing back by the entrance. "Um ... are you sure we're allowed to be in there?"

"Of course, we're allowed; it's public property. Cemeteries are actually nice places to visit — I come whenever I can. And I thought you might want to see where so many of the original inhabitants of Thornhill were buried."

"Um ... okay," I said. But my feet refused to move. This didn't feel right to me at all. Cemeteries weren't places you could just wander into for a stroll, were they? This would only be the second time in my life I'd ever been to a cemetery. The first time, of course, was at Papa's funeral last year. I shuffled my feet on the pavement, trying to decide what to do.

Caroline's lips twisted with amusement while she waited for me to start moving. "Wow, you're not afraid of this place, are you? Don't worry ... I'll protect you."

That did it! "No! Of course I'm not afraid!" I barked, forcing my feet toward the collection of gravestones. Keeping slightly ahead, Caroline led the way through the cemetery while I followed behind.

We were the only people there, as it was still very early on a Wednesday morning. It was quiet and surprisingly peaceful. There were trees all around, their swaying branches filled with chirping birds. The path was paved with a mosaic of flickering sunlight that shone down through the sparse leaves still remaining overhead. Every now and then, a little black squirrel would leap out from behind a gravestone and scurry across the path, as if playing a game of hide-and-seek. It was so calm and quiet that after a while I was almost able to forget that we were walking over a field of dead bodies.

Almost, but not quite. Because each stone called out its owner's name as we passed by.

Arnold, Bowes, Ramsden, Ness, Chapman — men, women, and children whose lives were cut off a long time ago, but whose names lived on in this quiet corner of town. Believe it or not, it was a strangely comforting place to be. Like a small corner of the world where immortality existed.

It took us about fifteen minutes to walk down the length of the path and back again. When we found ourselves back at the iron gateway, Caroline shook her head and sighed.

"I should probably get to work now. Nana will be wondering where I am."

I didn't want her to go. But I couldn't think of anything I could say to stop her. So I just nodded.

"Okay … I'll walk you back."

Just then, a sudden breeze blew through the graveyard, pulling leaves from the trees and scattering them through the air like confetti. A fiery orange one landed near the top of Caroline's head, sticking at a funny angle out of her hair. I don't know what kind of tree it was from, but it was shaped like a large, round teardrop. I had a sudden urge to reach out and pluck it from her hair, but I held back. I knew if I did that, I probably wouldn't be able to stop myself from wanting to smooth her hair down. And then I would want to touch her skin … and lean close to smell her. And then, of course, I'd want to kiss her lips, her neck, the hollow of her throat … and somehow I had a feeling *that* wouldn't go over so well.

Get a freaking hold of yourself, Max! I clenched my hands into fists, letting my fingernails dig into the skin of my palms while I tried to pull back my runaway thoughts. Was I some kind of twisted sicko for wanting to kiss a girl so badly in the middle of a cemetery?

So instead, I just pretended that the leaf wasn't there at all as I walked her back to 10 Colborne Street. Trust me, it was just easier that way.

11 – John

It was the summer of 1888 and Thornhill was growing at a fast clip. The first telephone in the village was
installed that year over at the Lindsay-Francis Store on
Yonge Street. For a small sum of money, a person could
conduct a long-distance telephone conversation with
another person as far south as the city of York. It was a
miraculous invention. I must admit, I was secretly envious for I'd always wanted to invent a machine just as
miraculous in my lifetime. Something like a flying ship.
Or a train that could travel underwater. But the long
days in the forge didn't allow much time for inventions.
Of course, for my father, the arrival of the telephone
was just another fine excuse to grumble about machines
and the disastrous advances of science. That man could
find the smallest spot in even the rosiest of apples.

Lure

That summer, I was fourteen and William was sixteen — both of us growing bigger by the hour. Certainly, we weren't children anymore, but we weren't quite adults, either. The purgatory of adolescence was upon us. And yet, because we were still so young and naive, neither of us had any idea that we were both careening toward the edge of a precipice. If only we'd been able to see it coming, things might have worked out differently. But of course, most mortals just aren't equipped with that kind of extraordinary foresight.

I find it quite ironic that I only came to possess that gift in the spirit realm, where it can't do me any good.

And so naturally, I had no way of knowing what kind of transformation had taken over my cousin during the winter months. When William arrived off the train that humid afternoon in early July, it was clear that everything about him had changed. I remember cringing at the sight of him. William had grown half a foot over the year since his last visit and must have stood close to six feet tall by my cursory estimation. He was a veritable giant! To make matters worse, I could see the outline of his newly broadened shoulders poking through his clothes and the dark stain of a full beard pushing through his once-smooth face. My cousin had transformed into a man over the course of the year. Just looking at him made my heart feel like it was sinking into my guts.

I knew that, like me, Father noticed the difference in William immediately, because his face broke into a wide grin at the sight of him. A strange sense of foreboding gripped me as I watched William search the sea of faces. A sudden impulse seized me — more than anything, I wanted to rush forward, push my cousin back onto the train, and send him straight home to Kingston. But it was too late to act on the impulse, for a second later he spotted us and was striding in our direction, his trademark smirk glued to his lips, his cap pulled rakishly down over his brow, and his bag slung across his shoulder like a hunting prize. Father leapt forward, grabbed William's hand and pumped it up and down vigorously, in exactly the same fashion that he might greet a fellow tradesman.

"It's good to have you back with us again, son," he boomed. I winced again. I couldn't ever remember a time when Father had addressed me as his son in the same prideful manner. The two of them strode off together while I trailed behind. I followed them across the road to the stagecoach with my head hanging low. In every possible way, it was clear to me that William was growing up while I remained just a child. Not knowing what I wanted in life or how to get it.

Lure

I'd never felt so miserable.

But that changed somewhat during the long ride back to 10 Colborne Street when William caught my eye and shot me a devilish wink the first moment Father's head was turned. Believe it or not, I felt instantly better knowing that there was a part of him still childish enough to want to terrorize me. I started imagining what mishaps the coming months would have in store for me. You would think with all the trouble William caused for me each summer, I'd tell my mother to stop inviting him to stay with us. Although she felt a strong duty to her nephew, she would put a halt to the visits without hesitation if I asked. But the truth is — I was lonely. And when William was there, I wasn't. One plus one equals two. It was as simple as that.

Before you get the wrong idea, I must confess that our relationship wasn't all cunning and plotting. Certainly, we had some good times together, too. There was the forge, of course. Having another person there to break up the long awkward silences between me and Father was a blessing. And on days when we weren't working, William and I sometimes played cards or took the horses for a run up Yonge Street. But by far, our favourite pastime was fishing in the Don River and the various mill ponds along its banks. Sometimes on a hot, windless day we'd sit on the shore and dangle our feet in the dark green water. Or, if no other person was near, we'd tear off our shirts, dip our hair in the pond and then straighten up and let the cool water drip down over our sweaty bodies. As tempted as William and I were to jump in when the weather turned hot, neither of us could swim worth a lick. So we did our best to stay cool along the shoreline.

The afternoon that William first hooked Sir John A. was one of those hot, windless days. Let me be clear from the start that I am referring to a fish, not our country's honourable first prime minister.

It was a Sunday. After church that morning, we returned home to change our clothes and fetch our fishing poles. Then we headed off to the Don. As usual, we cut through several neighbouring fields to get to the river that afternoon. Along the way we stopped to dig up some juicy worms and after we'd each collected a handful, we stuck them into our pockets so they couldn't escape. Along the way, we talked about trying our luck in one of the mill ponds, where we'd seen some bigger fish jumping the previous week. I recalled that it was the pond with the big willow tree at the south end, bent over like an old grandfather with the tips of its branches just grazing the ground.

Lure

Once William and I located the pond, we threaded the wriggling worms onto our hooks and then, as we often did when we went fishing, we separated from one another in order to keep our lines from crossing and getting tangled in the water.

"You take the north side, I'll take the south," William directed, turning and disappearing through the forest of tall reeds. I waited for a moment, listening to the crunch of his footsteps growing fainter with every step until finally they were too far away to hear. Then, dutifully, I headed off to my end of the pond. My hopes were to catch a big carp that day and present it to my parents for their dinner. But in the back of my head, I knew that William was probably hatching a similar plot. Fishing with my cousin was always a competition. Who would bring home the bigger catch and earn my father's praise? In previous years, my cousin was always the one to catch the biggest fish. But, to everyone's surprise, I'd been holding my own with William this summer.

And there are no words to describe to you how I relished the notion of the considerable irritation that brought to his life.

I cast my line out into the dark water and watched the worm sink slowly down until it was out of my sight. Then, taking a seat on a nearby rock, I pulled back and forth on the line to keep the worm from settling on the muddy bottom of the pond. A big, blue dragonfly flitted across the rippling water, its wings shimmering in the afternoon sunlight. The pointed tips of the surrounding reeds swayed and sighed in the soft breeze.

"Come on, fish," I sang out. "Come get your lunch." I held my breath and waited, but the croaking of a nearby frog was the only reply. Either the fish on my end of the pond weren't hungry or my singing scared them off, for I didn't even get one nibble that afternoon. Lady Luck, however, had chosen to smile upon my cousin. About twenty minutes after we'd first separated, I heard him bellowing from the other side of the pond.

"John! I've got one!"

Now normally that kind of announcement wouldn't be any reason for concern. But there was an uncharacteristic urgency in William's voice that raised the hairs on the back of my neck. In a trice, I dropped my own pole and dashed off toward the south end of the pond.

"John, come quick!" William's voice surged across the water again. "And get the net!"

"I'm coming!"

I pushed through the overgrowth of reeds, trying to run as fast as I could without slipping on the green, spongy ground. When I finally reached William, however, I found that there was no need for the net. The battle was clearly over. He was collapsed on the bank, pole at his side, and streams of sweat running down his face. He was scowling ferociously in the direction of the water, his broad chest heaving with exertion. I stared at him in shock. My big strong cousin had lost to a *fish*?

"What happened?" I called out, rushing to his side. It was a strange feeling to see William looking so vulnerable.

"I had him on the line, but he was too powerful," he explained, his words emerging slowly between each panting breath. "I thought he'd drag me into the pond with him, he was that big. I held on to him for a minute and managed to pull him toward me when he got away. He even broke my pole."

And here he held up the remains of his fishing pole, snapped off in the middle by the treacherous fish. Suddenly, I felt like laughing. In an effort to conceal my smirk, I looked out onto the water, searching for signs of the struggle. The pond was smooth as glass, save for the lonely head of a small painted turtle peeking through the surface for a breath of air.

"What kind of fish was he?" I asked, desperate to imagine the scaly beast that had conquered William. Could he hear the smile hiding behind my words?

"I don't know ... maybe a carp, possibly a northern pike. But it was certainly the biggest fish I have ever hooked. He must have weighed close to twenty pounds. He was enormous!"

It was difficult to imagine the mill pond sustaining a fish of that size, but I held my tongue. Tossing his broken pole to the side, William rose to his feet.

"Yes, Sir John A. was certainly the biggest fish I have ever hooked," he repeated, slapping the mud from his hands with a series of loud claps.

Sir John A.? That just wouldn't do!

"Pardon me, William ... but don't you think it's blasphemous to name a fish after our prime minister?"

He frowned and let out a crude, swine-like snort. "Blasphemous? Don't be stupid, little cousin."

"But he's been granted a knighthood," I argued, ignoring his coarseness. "Under the order of Her Majesty, Queen Victoria, no less. To give a fish the same name ..."

"... is a show of respect," he cut in. "Why shouldn't every great leader have a great name? And after all, Sir John A. is the biggest, most powerful fish in the pond."

I stopped talking, for how could I argue with that reasoning? I watched in silence as William picked up the remains of his broken pole and flung them into the water. After that, he didn't want to fish anymore.

"I need a new pole and Sir John A. needs a break to gather his strength back," he said. "It just wouldn't be fair to go after him again so soon."

I imagined perhaps it was really William who needed the strength-gathering break, but I kept that thought to myself.

"Fine, we'll come back next week after church," I replied. "We can try to get him then."

The sun was just beginning to make its way down from the height of the sky. William and I leaned lazily back among the tall reeds and stared up into the cloudless ceiling above us. A family of mallard ducks napped under the shade of the willow tree, their bills nestled under their wings like little children tucked snugly into their beds.

A cicada buzzed loudly somewhere nearby.

"Do you know that there's a girl back in Kingston with eyes that exact colour of blue?" William whispered, pointing upwards. I turned to look at him in shock. Why did his voice suddenly sound so hoarse? It was as if there was something caught in his throat.

"Her name is Martha Henry and she's got the most beautiful eyes you've ever seen," he continued, slowly lowering his hand. "Bluer than that sky. And hair brighter than sunlight on the water."

My brow pleated with concentration as I tried so

hard to imagine eyes like he described. A second later, I heard the dried reeds rustle under William's head as he turned toward me.

"Martha's family lives in the house next door to mine. Perhaps you remember meeting her that summer you visited Kingston?"

My thoughts flew back to that summer. I could vaguely recall the memory of a golden-haired girl who had found me crouched behind a raspberry thicket during a neighbourhood game of hide-and-seek. She'd looked to be a few years older than me and had a face so lovely and sweet that I remember thinking it belonged on a church stained-glass window. Could that have been Martha Henry?

"Can you keep a secret, John?" William continued.

A secret? I nodded dumbly and waited to hear what he had to say. It was the first and only time my cousin had ever confided in me.

"I kissed Martha last winter. I kissed her twice, actually. She was incredibly ... soft."

Soft? An odd feeling started to grow in the pit of my stomach. It was like a small flame that was growing, expanding like a wildfire until I felt my whole face and neck begin to burn with the heat. My imagination stretched across the space between us to catch up to his thoughts.

"Which part of her was so soft?"

He smiled a secretive, smug smile. And then his deep voice lowered to a light murmur, as if he was confessing to a priest. "She was soft all over. Her hair, her lips, her skin, her ..." His voice trailed off into deafening silence. My mind spun.

"Go on," I whispered, my heart already quickening at the suggestion behind his silence. "Go on." But as much as I tried to get him to say more, he flatly refused. Instead, he simply closed his eyes and sighed. There was the tiniest of smiles resting upon his face, as if he were enjoying the memory of a good book or listening to someone playing a nocturne on the piano.

"And what does this girl Martha Henry think of a boy with fingers as black as coal from working in the forge?" I asked, my words barbed with envy.

But William didn't reply. And his smile didn't fade for a second.

How infuriating!

Snapping a reed from the patch beside me, I held it between my thumbs and began to whistle a tune. Then I closed my eyes and tried to imagine touching, feeling, kissing something as soft as William's words were suggesting. Would any part of Harriet Miller, the girl who had sat beside me at school, feel soft if I had ever dared to reach a petrified hand out to touch her? Or Kate, our family's hired girl? Kate was probably twenty years old by now, but the thought of her red skin and chapped hands made me doubt that any part of her could compare to what my cousin was describing.

Until that point, the softest thing I'd ever touched in my life was the little lamb Father had accepted as payment for fixing the broken lock on Thomas Hamill's gate. I was a few days shy of my seventh birthday when Father had brought it home and let me pat it for a few minutes outside in the back garden while he searched for his whetstone. I can remember how it trembled with fright as I held it in my arms. It wasn't much bigger than a cat. While I patted its soft fur, I silently prayed that Mother would come home and intervene before Father finished sharpening his knife. The lamb's eyes were large and dark and scared and I was certain that it was aware on some primal level of what was about to happen. So I leaned down and whispered a church hymn in its trembling ear to keep it calm in those final minutes of its life. It smelled of grass and sunshine and outside. Somehow, I managed to hold back my tears when Father pried it away from me, carried it into the barn, and butchered it for our evening meal. I wouldn't join my parents for dinner that night. Instead, I stayed upstairs weeping in the privacy of my bedroom where Father couldn't scold me for behaving like a sentimental girl. I remember feeling so angry at Mother for being gone that evening that I didn't speak to her for the rest of the night. If she'd been home, she never would have let Father slaughter that poor little animal.

That lamb was the softest thing I'd ever known. Could any part of this girl Martha Henry have been softer than the pale, silky curls on that lamb's belly? I wanted to know. But at the same time, I was also glad that William had stopped talking. Part of me was afraid that if he continued, the fire inside me would burn through my skin and fry my body until nothing was left. Cases of spontaneous combustion had been documented before. What if it was about to happen to me? Would William have the sense to douse the flames with water from the pond? Or would he simply allow me to ignite here amidst the reeds and smoulder away to ashes? I bit my lip and waited to see what William would say next. But he remained stubbornly silent on the subject of Martha Henry. Could he see how his story of this girl had burned my face? Perhaps he realized he'd gone too far by telling me so much. Or perhaps it was I who'd gone too far.

The bells of the church chimed in the distance, bringing my daydreams back to reality.

Bong, bong, bong, bong.

Four o'clock. It was approaching the dinner hour. Leaving my cousin alone with his thoughts, I crept out of the reeds to retrieve my fishing pole.

I stewed about William's selfish secrecy for days. But, in the end, I forgave him for his silence. Especially when I found out that William had decided that Martha Henry was the girl he was going to marry. He would be turning seventeen in a few more months and was starting to think about these things. Yes, William was almost grown up. He was making plans for his future, his profession, and a family of his own. And here I was, still a child — going through life with my head in the sand.

Unseeing and unseen.

12 – Max

I was reading a book when the first wet letter appeared.

It happened while I was studying in the deserted back room of the library. By then, it was the second week in October and I was still coming back to Colborne Street every Wednesday morning, eager for the chance to be near Caroline. Even though it was pretty obvious that she didn't think of me as anything more than a weird, lonely kid, I couldn't stay away from her. I'd even gone as far as officially dropping my Wednesday-morning class so I could keep the teachers and parentals off my back about the ditching. I know, it was desperate and sad … but I couldn't seem to stop myself. She was everything I thought about all day long. And at night, the image of her eyes and smile haunted my dreams. I admit it — I was a total head case.

It was while I was scanning through my science textbook that the wet letter materialized with painstaking slowness on the left hand side of the page — almost as if it was being drawn by the wet finger of a distracted child. Although at that moment, I didn't realize it was a letter because it just looked like a long, quivery line.

At first, I didn't think anything of it. In fact, my only instinct was to check the ceiling to see if I was sitting under a leaky spot. I knew from working with my grandfather how notoriously porous these old buildings could be. I glanced up, but the ceiling looked smooth and dry ... not a leak in sight. The water had to be coming from somewhere else.

Staring back down at the wet book, my imagination began leaping in all directions like a frog chasing a frantic fly. But I refused to let it veer off in the one direction I knew it would eventually take.

No, Max ... don't go there! Do. Not. Go. There.

Trying to distract myself from my own thoughts, I flipped the wet page and forced myself to continue with my reading as if nothing had happened. That's when the second wet letter appeared. I watched in horror as a very distinct "s" slowly formed in a long, watery squiggle on the page.

What the hell?

Lure

A cold chill passed over my skin ... like someone had just turned the A/C on full blast beside me. Feeling a scream rise in my throat, I hurled the book to the floor and jumped to my feet. My heart felt like it was about to pound out of my chest. It was taking all my willpower to keep the scream from escaping my lips. I looked around me to see if Caroline was anywhere in sight, but the back room of the library was deserted as usual. I was totally alone. My instincts were telling me to run away and never come back. But my curiosity was getting the better of my instincts.

What the hell was going on?

I had to know.

After a deep breath or two, I felt calm enough to pick the book back up and take another look. Holding it as carefully as a stick of dynamite, I thumbed through the pages until I found the wet letter. Yup, there was no mistaking it. It was definitely an "s." I ran my shaking fingers over the page while my brain wrestled with the only conclusion it could find.

Crap! It's the ghosts! One of them is here with me. In this room ... right now.

And in that moment, I believed it all. Every word of every crazy ghost story Caroline had told me. I don't know why I didn't just drop everything and get out of there. It probably would have been the rational thing to do. But when the book in your hands suddenly becomes haunted by the spirit of some long-gone dead soul, can you blame a guy for not thinking rationally? So instead of running away, I did something really, *really* stupid. I flipped the page over to see what would happen next. Instantly, a third wet letter appeared. This was very clearly a lower case "e."

And on the next page, another "e."

"Isee"? No, it's "I see." It's a message! Holy crap, the ghost is writing me a message!

"What do you see?" I whispered, turning another page. The letters were coming faster and faster now, like a train picking up speed. A few more seconds and a few more flips and the rest of the sentence was complete.

IseeyouMax

Oh my God!

This time, I was too freaked out to even think about screaming. It was just like Caroline had said the other day ... like my voice had been grabbed from my throat. And my brain was all clogged up with one word that was playing over and over like a broken record.

Ghost ... ghost ... ghost ...

I could feel my blood racing through my veins as my heart pumped wildly with panic. Although there were no windows open in the library that morning, another cold breeze suddenly passed over my neck and my skin exploded with a cover of icy tingles. I shook my head to chase them away. They ran up my scalp and escaped out the roots of my hair.

And then, strangely, I was calm again. Eerily calm.

Looking up from the book, I stole a quick glance around the room. I don't know what I was looking for exactly. A smoky figure hovering above me? A scary lady in a calico skirt and high-button boots? Or maybe something sinister and ghastly like a scene out of a horror movie? But the room was totally empty. Wherever the ghost was, it hadn't decided to show itself to me. But I did have the wet book in my hands — it was the proof I'd been asking for all along.

Show this to Caroline, a silent voice inside my brain shouted. *She'll want to see the letters.*

Desperately, I started turning the pages back, trying to find the beginning of the ghost's message. But it was as if the book had swallowed them up because every single one of those wet letters was gone, dried up like disappearing ink.

The book fell open into my lap as I slumped back against the couch. There was no proof. Absolutely nothing to show Caroline. I was such an idiot. I should have called her over sooner. Or taken the book with me and gone to find her. And then a crazy thought crossed my mind. The letters were gone now ... but had they even been there in the first place? Or had I just been seeing things? Or worse, imagining that I was seeing things? Holy crap, this place was messing with my mind!

I dropped my head into my hands and let out a low, frustrated moan as I stared into the open pages of the damned book. And then for the second time, it started to happen. As I watched in amazement, another wet letter began to form on the page sitting open on my lap. This one was an upper case "D."

A new message ...

I ran my finger over the page, trying to convince myself that I wasn't just imagining it. Yeah, it sure felt like wet paper. When I raised the tip of my finger to my nose and took a sniff, I immediately recognized the same swampy smell I'd been covered with the other morning in my bed. No, this definitely wasn't in my head! Bolting upright, I started flipping the pages again, trying to keep up with the latest sequence of wet scribbles. This time, there were only nine letters ... but the message was unmistakably clear.

Donottell

Oh man! The pain was so bad! It was like someone was gripping my heart in their fist. I held back a scream as my eyes flew around the room, hoping to make contact with the ghost. "Okay, okay ... I won't tell," I whispered into the empty air. "I promise, I won't tell anyone." As soon as I got those words out, the clenching pain in my chest began to ease up. Relief covered me like a soft blanket. "But I just want to know," I added, still gasping from the ordeal, "W-who are you?"

More wet letters soaked the pages.

Ilivedherelongago

"And ... are you the ghost of Ellen Ramsden?"

NoIamJohn

John? A man? I shook my head, suddenly even more confused than before. But how did that explain those apparitions? The skirt, the moaning old lady, the woman in the window?

"Which John were you?" I asked, remembering what Caroline had said the previous week. I held my breath and waited for his answer to appear on the pages. Was I about to solve the mysterious identity of the library ghost? My palms started to sweat with panicky excitement and I had to move them away from the book so I wouldn't blur the answer. I sat like a statue, waiting for the letters to come. But for a full five minutes there was nothing. Nothing but silence and the dry book in my lap.

Did I ask the wrong thing? Did I scare the ghost away? Or piss him off somehow?

And then finally, just when I was about to close the book and leave, a series of very shaky letters slowly began to appear on the pages. They spelled out:

Ineedyourhelp

I sucked my breath in so sharply, I almost choked on the air. John wanted *my* help? For what? Did he want me to commit unearthly deeds? To help him with his haunting? To smoke a butt with him in the stairwell?

"W-what do you want me to do?"

This time, the letters came at lightning speed — almost faster than I could turn the pages to read them.

Iwantmylureback

13 — John

It all came to a boil in late August of 1889. That was the summer when I was fifteen and William was seventeen — the hottest summer anybody in Thornhill could ever remember. That was the summer when mosquitoes ruled the evening sky, wasps swarmed around us like enemy armies, and the air was so thick and sticky it was like breathing through a bowl of porridge.

That was also the summer that my weak, skinny body finally began to show signs of maturing. I had grown quickly over the winter months, which had forced my mother to let out all the hems in my pants and shirts. By the time summer had arrived, I was gaining on William's height, although he was still much broader and heavier than me. In addition, my once-boyish voice had recently begun to take on a rough, raspy quality which I knew meant it would begin to deepen soon. My insides ached with pride every time I heard myself speak. Yes, I was fully aware that my feelings were foolish and vain, but yet I couldn't contain my excitement at the sound of those gravelly words coming from my lips. Each one a proclamation to the world that I was growing up.

And yet, at the same time, there was a piece of my heart that was dreading the end of my childhood. As uncomfortable as that hot summer was, I didn't want it to ever end. You see, that year was to be the end of William's time with us in Thornhill. He was engaged to be married to Martha Henry in October. Preparations were underway for their future together. They would be living in a house of their own by the following summer and opening up their own blacksmith shop in Kingston.

With William going off to get married, I would be alone with my father in the forge and on my own to face the responsibilities of my life. Yes, the year I turned fifteen was the year that promised to change everything. And it all started with the lure.

Back in June of that summer, my mother had given me not one, but two, gifts for the occasion of my birthday. There was the annual secret book, of course, which she had slipped under my pillow the night before so I would awake to the happy discovery of the newest addition to my collection. I had five of my own books by that point, all of them shelved safely away from my father's grasp at the home of my old schoolteacher, Mr. Brown, with whom I kept a regular correspondence.

Imagine my excitement when I pulled back my pillow to find a detective mystery novel. This year, Mother had ordered me a newly published work entitled *A Study in Scarlet* written by an Englishman named Arthur Conan Doyle. Although I'd never heard anything about this particular author, I concluded before I'd even finished reading the first page that it was going to be a wonderful book. And, indeed, it was. It was also the last book I would ever own (although I must confess that I've been fortunate enough to have read an entire library worth of texts over the ensuing years).

My mother's second birthday gift was not given to me in secret, however. In fact, she presented it to me after dinner that night, right in front of Father and William. As she handed the wrapped box to me, conversation came to a halt. The air around our dining table suddenly swelled with an uneasy silence. I stared at it for a moment, stunned by her audacity. It was a little box wrapped in delicate blue paper and topped with one of the summer's first roses that she had clipped from the garden at the side of the house. I held it in my hands, unsure what to do next. I could only imagine what sort of awful thoughts were coursing through my father's head in that moment.

"Well, aren't you going to open it, my love?" I heard my mother ask.

I nodded. A flush of nervous heat was beginning to spread across my face. My fingers shook as I peeled apart the wrapper, for I could feel Father's disapproving glare weighing upon me from across the table. What I discovered inside the little box stole the next breath from my body. There, nestled on a ball of white cotton, was a fishing lure. It was a spoon lure, with four separate spinners and a bright orange feather attached to the end. Just one look at it and I could imagine it twirling through the water, catching the light from above like the scales of a fish. With a sharp gasp, I reached in and stroked the orange feather slowly and carefully, worried that my clumsy fingers might crush it if they moved too fast. It was the most incredible thing anyone had ever given me. Dare I say it was even better than my precious books? The sharp prick of oncoming tears stung my eyes, but I swallowed hard to banish any sign of weakness before Father's keen gaze could spot it. I looked up at my mother, searching for a way to thank her without surrendering to my emotions. She must have sensed the difficulty I was having, for she immediately came to my rescue.

"You're welcome, John," she said, speaking first so I wouldn't have to. Her lips were pressed into the tiniest of smiles. "I purchased it from Mr. Ostertag's shop. You've been admiring his lures for so long now."

I nodded again. Mr. Ostertag was a local tinsmith whose shop was across the street from the forge. Inside his shop were all sorts of wonderful items that he'd created from tin: kitchenware, decorative boxes, tools, candle holders, and toys (even an army of tin soldiers like Frankie Wilson's). And, of course, the fishing lures. In the years since I began working in the forge, I would often wander into his shop during my brief lunch breaks to admire the display of lures Mr. Ostertag kept inside a large glass case near the back counter. But I'd never once dreamed of having one of my own.

"Thank you," I finally managed to say when my emotions had been brought well under control. Out of the corner of my eye, I saw my father scowl as I leaned across the table and placed a grateful kiss upon Mother's cheek. I could hear his thoughts just as clearly as if he were shaking me by the shoulders and shouting them in my face.

You are spoiling the boy with such an extravagant gift! His mind should be focused on working on the forge and not on idle pastimes like fishing!

I avoided his eyes for the rest of the evening, determined not to let him ruin my fifteenth birthday with his dark mood. So intent was I on evading Father's wrath, I didn't even notice that my cousin William was being unusually silent that night. Nor did I notice the way his nose wrinkled as if there was something rotten beneath it when I removed the lure from its box to admire it from a closer angle. Yes, if only I had been more aware, fate might have played out differently that summer. But, there I go getting ahead of myself again.

As it was William's final summer in the village, he had vowed to catch Sir John A. before moving back to Kingston at the end of August. Certainly, I was happy to join him on this quest, for I was eager to take advantage of every fishing opportunity to try out my new lure. As a result, we found ourselves on the shores of the mill pond every weekend that summer. We planted ourselves among the reeds and rocks and we fished for hours — all day long, regardless of the cloud of heat that had fallen over the village. And of course, every time without fail, William asked to use my lure.

"Come, just once. I can show you how it's supposed to be done."

Lure

And every time without fail, I steadfastly refused. The lure was the most valuable thing I'd ever owned. I certainly wasn't going to take the chance of losing it by lending it to William. I must admit, I did have another reason to keep the lure for myself. As you might imagine, I was secretly hoping to catch the prize fish for myself and win what was most certainly to be the final competition with my cousin.

I caught many fish that summer, as did William. But Sir John A. continued to elude our fishing lines.

"Perhaps he's dead?" I suggested at the end of a long, hot afternoon as we dragged our feet back up the muddy road toward home.

"Stupid!" replied William, slapping me across the shoulder. "Sir John A. is the biggest fish in this pond. Who could kill him?"

"Well, perhaps somebody else has caught him, then?"

But we both knew that was unlikely. There was nobody else in the village foolish enough to spend those terribly hot days chasing after a silly fish. Nobody but me and William.

14 – Max

A *lure?* Like … a fishing lure? Were fishing lures even invented back in those olden days?

I admit, I was kind of disappointed. Call me slow, but I couldn't understand why a ghost would be making the effort to contact me from the "other side" about a stupid thing like a fishing lure? Maybe there was a different meaning to the word back then. Or maybe it was made out of gold or diamonds or something. I wanted to ask John why he cared about it so much, but stopped myself before the words could come out. If it were possible for a ghost to be sensitive, this one clearly was. And the last thing I wanted to do was piss him off again. So in the end I just agreed.

"Sure, I'll help you get your lure back," I whispered

to the empty room. "Just tell me where you want me to look."

One by one, the wet letters slithered through the pages of the book.

Itsburiedinthegarden

The garden? That was a pretty big area to search for something so small. I needed him to be more specific if I was going to find it. "Okay. *Where* in the garden?"

I kept my eyes glued to the pages and waited for his answer. Nothing happened. I waited for a long time, almost afraid to move so I wouldn't scare him away. But there was no response at all.

Crap! I must have upset him again.

Just when I thought that I'd gone and scared him off for good, I felt a sudden breeze brush by my face. And then there was a loud creak and a bang, like the sound of the front door opening and closing. The hairs on my arms rose up like an army of soldiers standing to attention. Jumping to my feet, I raced to the library door.

"Did you see someone just walk out of there?" I asked Caroline's grandmother, pausing for a second by the front desk. She shook her head, the folds in her neck swinging like curtains.

"Speak up, young man. And stop running in this

library." Her words were slick with disapproval. Okay, *whatever!*

A moment later, Caroline walked out of the parlour carrying an armload of books.

"Hey, did you just see someone leave the library?" I demanded. Her eyes grew big with surprise; two giant blue marbles.

"Why are you still here, Max? I thought you'd left for school already."

I darted over to her side and lowered my head so that our faces were just inches apart. It was hard, but I managed to force myself to ignore her delicious smell. "Listen to me very carefully," I commanded. "Did you see anybody walk out of the library in the last minute or two?"

All of the colour slowly drained out of her cheeks. "W-what are you talking about?" she asked. "Don't tell me you're seeing ghosts now, too?"

I didn't know how to answer that question without breaking my promise to John. So, I just pretended like I didn't even hear it. "Forget it. I gotta go."

Charging past her, I threw open the door and headed outside. The sunshine hit me like a punch in the face. It was so bright, I had to cover my eyes to see properly. I walked around the garden, searching for ... I didn't know exactly. A person? A ghost? A man with a fishing pole? But there was no one there. The gardens were empty and quiet. The buzz of a nearby cricket, the soft hush of leaves blowing in the wind, and the low hum of morning traffic from nearby Yonge Street were the only sounds around. When I reached the back of the house, I turned and slowly began to walk back in the direction I came from. The garden was completely deserted.

Idiot! Who exactly did you think you were chasing out here?

And then suddenly to my left, there was a rapid rustling sound like the crumpling of dry leaves. A moment later, a little black squirrel darted out from behind a patch of balsam and ran in front of me. My eyes followed him as he rushed down the garden path. That's when I noticed the circular puddle of water slowly spreading across the pavement next to my shoes. I froze, my arms and legs like blocks of petrified wood.

Where's the water coming from? Thornhill hasn't had rain in over a week.

When I was finally able to regain control of my limbs, I crouched down low, put my nose to the puddle, and sniffed. Yeah, I probably looked like a lunatic. I'm sure that anyone passing by at that moment would have thought I'd lost my mind. And, who knows, maybe I had. All I knew for sure was that the puddle had a definite swampy smell to it. Which could only mean one thing.

The ghost was here in the garden!

With my pulse pounding in my ears, I yanked back the foliage and searched through the overgrown remains of the summer garden. A moment later I found what I was looking for. There, etched into a cleared patch of dirt, was a very distinct letter X.

John had marked the exact spot for me to dig up his lure.

It took me a couple of seconds to find my breath.

Okay, Einstein … what are you going to do now? Go find a shovel and start digging? Right here in broad daylight?

I knew if someone saw me, I'd get in a lot of trouble … maybe even arrested. This wasn't just an ordinary house, after all. It was an historic property. And the garden was a … what did Caroline call it again? Oh yeah, a heritage garden. She'd said it was built and protected by the town. No, I would have to get permission to dig here. The only problem was that John very clearly told me not to talk to anyone about this. Just the memory of that moment brought back a flash of squeezing pain in my chest. Okay, I had to think of another way.

The first thing I needed to do was talk to Caroline. Slapping the dirt from my hands, I headed back to the side entrance of the library. She was coming out just as I was going in. Her face was still pale as a snowdrift.

"What's going on?" she demanded, her eyes searching my face for clues. "Why did you run out of here like that? Are you okay?" There was a sadness in her eyes and voice — it almost looked like she was about to cry. Wow, she really *did* care about me. What a real friend she was turning out to be. Except I didn't want her as my friend. I wanted so much more. How freakin' frustrating!

"Yeah, everything's fine. I just thought I heard a noise, but I was wrong." *Man, it was frightening how easily I could spew out these lies.* "Sorry if I worried you," I added after a second. *That part, at least, was the truth.*

But I could tell from the scrunch of her eyebrows that she was still concerned about what had just happened. With a sigh, she gestured back toward the library door. "Okay, well, you left your science book in the back room when you ran out here. Aren't you going to need it for school this afternoon?"

My insides twisted with pain; like someone was wringing out all my vital organs. *The science text with all of John's swampy messages.* Crap! Had Caroline

flipped through it? Had she seen any of the wet letters? Did she somehow figure out what was going on?
I wanted to tell her what had happened so much, it
hurt to keep it inside. But I had to make myself do it. I
didn't want to put her in any kind of danger by telling
her what I'd seen.

"Oh, um ... thanks," I replied, forcing my voice
to stay cool. "I *do* need it for school, today. I'll go
get it in a sec ... um ..." My brain scrambled for a
way to change the subject. "So, I was wondering ...
do you think it would it be okay if I wanted to do
some, well, a bit of gardening work out here? The
grounds look like they could use a bit of weeding
and maintenance."

By the look on her face, you'd think I'd just suggested we run away together and elope in Las Vegas.

"You want to start digging around in our garden?"

I nodded and smiled, hoping I could somehow act
charming enough to pull this one off.

"Are you sure about that? It's October. The growing season is over."

"Yeah, I know, but the beds could use some prep
work for the winter."

She shot me a strange look, like I was some kind
of a tricky math problem she was trying to work out
in her head. "I think it's a great idea, but we already

have a gardener, you know. He comes every couple of weeks."

Wow, this girl could argue! If she ever did make it to university, she could be one hell of a good lawyer. But I could give back as good as I got. Turning to the side, I waved my hand over an especially thick patch of prickly looking weeds. "Yeah, well, maybe you should be looking for a new gardener. Whoever you've hired is doing a lousy job out here."

Suddenly, Caroline's hands rose up onto her hips and her elbows cut through the air. *Uh-oh! Made her mad!*

"Excuse me, but this is a heritage garden. What makes you think you're so qualified to care for it, anyway?"

Her words were short, clipped, and defensive. Yup, she was angry. Guess I shouldn't be surprised … she was pretty protective of this property. Maybe I shouldn't have insulted the garden like that. I wasn't pulling off the charming thing so well. It was time for a different approach.

"Please, Caroline, if you could just look into it for me, I'd be really grateful. I love this kind of work … it would be cool to help in such an important garden."

Her hands slowly slipped off her hips and fell to her sides. *Okay … that's better!*

"Well, it's not going to be easy to get permission," she said with a sigh. "This place is protected by the town, so you could get in a lot of trouble if you don't go through the proper channels. I'd like to help, but I really think Nana is the best person to ask about it."

Nana? I smiled as I thanked her, but my heart was quietly sinking into my shoes. It was so obvious that her grandmother didn't like me one bit. She'd *never* give me permission to dig out here.

My eyes shot over to where the secret X was lying, hidden behind the patch of withering balsam. Helping this ghost was going to be harder than I thought. But I figured by that point, John had been waiting a long time to get his lure back. Hopefully, he wouldn't mind waiting a little bit longer.

15 – John

Strong hands grabbed me by the shoulders and shook me awake.

"Get up!"

I turned over and peered through the blackness.

"William?"

"Get out of bed, John!"

"W-what time is it?"

The hands shook me again, harder this time. "It's half past four in the morning. Come now, get up."

I shut my eyes and groaned. "Leave me alone. I'm tired."

A moment later, my quilt was flying off my body with a forceful yank.

"It's time to wake up," William's voice hissed above me. "We're going fishing."

I sat up in bed, shivering from the cool night air. My eyes flicked to the window. Nothing but blackness seeped through the narrow slats of the shutters.

"Are you mad? It's much too dark out there for fishing."

But clearly, William didn't agree. He marched over to my dresser and threw open the drawers. "Don't be stupid, John! In all those books you've claimed to have read, have you never learned that fish bite best at dawn?" He turned back to me and tossed an armful of clothes onto my lap. "Now get dressed and stop wasting time."

I rubbed the sleep out of my eyes and shook my head to clear my foggy brain. What was William's hurry? Why was he so determined to wrest me from my bed? And then I remembered. Today was the final day of his summer visit. He was scheduled to travel back to Kingston on the twelve o'clock train and begin preparations for his wedding to Martha Henry.

While I struggled to dress myself in the darkness, William strode over and removed my fishing pole from the back corner of my room where I always kept it. "Won't you hurry, John? If there's any hope of catching Sir John A., we need to be casting our lines into the water well before the sun rises."

Ah! So that's what this was about! William didn't

want to leave for home without his prize fish. I hesitated with my shirt poised over my head, trying to decide what to do. There was a part of me that wanted to go fishing. With some luck, perhaps I could even catch Sir John A. out from under William's nose. My heart leapt at the thought of how jealous that would make him! But at the same time, I was nervous about soliciting my father's anger by sneaking out to fish on the morning of William's departure.

Still undecided, I brought the shirt down over my head. "Mother and Father would never approve of this. Have you forgotten that the stagecoach is arriving immediately after breakfast to take you to the train depot?"

"Don't fret, cousin. We'll return home in plenty of time for the carriage. It's still an hour to daybreak." He grasped my elbow and pulled me to my feet with surprising force. "But now's the time to go. All of the fish will be jumping soon."

He handed me my shoes. I bent down to slip them on. When I stood back up, there was a curious expression on William's face.

"Now where's the lure?"

Suddenly defensive, I crossed my arms in front of my chest like a shield. "No, I won't let you use it," I said. "It's my lure."

His expression broke into a smile. "Yes, of course it's yours. I just thought you would want to bring it with you to the pond this morning. Won't you be using it to catch Sir John A.?"

He had a good point.

"Well, all right …" I conceded, "… but first close your eyes."

William threw back his head and laughed. "What difference will it make if I discover your hiding place now? I'll be leaving forever in only a few more hours."

Nevertheless, I made him turn around and cover his eyes while I fetched my lure from its hiding place in the hollowed-out pine knot behind my headboard.

"Yes, I have it. You can look now," I said, clasping the lure tightly in my hand.

William smiled again and clapped me roughly on the shoulder. "Good fellow. Shall we go, then?"

I hesitated, sensing a problem with his plan. "But, how are we going to get out of the house without waking Mother and Father? If they hear us on the stairwell, they'll never let us go."

"Ah, but there's a simple solution for that," William replied, walking over to my bedroom window and pulling up the sash. "We just slide down the maple tree and sneak out through the back garden."

Lure

My cousin had surely taken leave of his senses. I didn't enjoy climbing up trees, let alone sliding down them. As the painful memories from our last window escapade flooded my mind, William pushed open the shutters, sat down on the frame and swung his legs around.

"No, wait …" I said, running to stop him. "I think I might have changed my mind about the fishing." But it was too late. William had already hopped out onto the nearest branch and was lowering himself down to the ground. He alighted easily and looked up to where I was still standing by the open window.

"Now throw me the poles and the lure," he called.

My fingers instinctively tightened around the lure. "Why?"

William's hands flew up in exasperation. "Why? So they won't break to pieces if you fall, you horse's ass!"

"I don't know about this … I don't think I like your plan very much."

I could just make out the silhouette of my cousin's foot tapping against the ground. "Come on, John," he persisted. "You're wasting time with this foolishness. It'll be morning soon, and we will have lost our last chance at that fish."

Shaking my head, I took a small step back from the window, trying to decide what I should do. Perhaps

William sensed his advantage beginning to wane, because he suddenly turned mean.

"Don't tell me you're afraid of climbing down that tree?" he asked, his voice raised into a taunting singsong. "Or perhaps it's the darkness that has you so scared? Shall I wake your mother so she can comfort you?"

With a sigh, I stepped forward and tossed the fishing poles out the window. William caught them easily enough, placed them side by side on the ground, and then raised his hands toward me.

"And now for the lure."

Against all my better judgment, I pulled it out from behind my back, took a calming breath, and let it fall, watching the fine orange feather flutter through the night air as it dropped toward the ground. William caught it easily in his outstretched hands.

"I've got it," I heard him say from below. Smiling, I finally let out that long-held breath. It was like all the muscles in my body suddenly relaxed the moment I knew that my lure was safe.

"All right — I'm coming down now," I announced, swinging my legs over the window frame. Instead of William's reply, however, all I heard was the crunching of shoes on the gravel pathway and the metallic clank of the gate shutting closed. Straining my eyes through the darkness, I caught the faint shadow of my cousin's form escaping up the road.

"Hey! Come back!"

Momentarily forgetting about my fear of heights, I leapt onto the branch, slid down the trunk of the maple tree, and took off after him. My pulse was drumming with anger as I dashed up the road to the mill pond. The ground was damp with dew and the muddy road squished beneath my shoes with every step.

What a dirty liar! How could I have not seen that William had been plotting to steal my lure all along? How could I have let him trick me again? And, worst of all, why hadn't I learned my lesson after all these years? I really was a fool! A veritable horse's ass!

By the time I arrived at the pond, my entire body was throbbing with fury. Panting from the run, I scanned the scene and quickly spied William standing beneath the old willow tree, his silhouette black against the glowing sky. The tip of his fishing pole was raised high in the air. There was no doubt in my mind that my lure was at the end of his line. Although it was still quite dark out, I was certain that I could discern the mocking expression on his face.

My fists were clenched tight with anger as I raced over to reclaim my stolen lure.

If I hadn't been so preoccupied with my cousin, I might have taken a moment to appreciate the beautiful sight of the pond in the pre-dawn hour. The air was humming with the night-time chorus of crickets. A layer of ghostly mist was rising off the water. And somewhere below the horizon, the sun was preparing to break into a new day.

If only I'd known that it was to be my last day alive.

16 – Max

Bureaucracy is a bitch.

I'd heard my dad say those words a million times when he was going through the frustrating process of looking for a new job last year ... the job that eventually ended up uprooting our lives and bringing us here to Thornhill. But as many times as I heard him say it, I never understood what he was talking about.

Until now, that is.

It felt like it was taking forever to get permission to dig in the garden. Two weeks had already gone by since I'd first asked Nana and still nothing. Caroline claimed she was trying her best to hurry her grandmother along, but as far as I knew, the paperwork hadn't even been filled out yet. By now, I could tell that Nana was getting tired of me asking about it, because she snapped at me whenever I tried to bring up the question.

I decided to try and take my mind off it by doing some research on fishing lures. I was no history expert, but I still was having a hard time believing that they would have been invented back in the olden days. When I Googled "old lures" I got lots of hits, but most of the websites looked a bit sketchy. So just to be sure, I decided to check out some books on the subject. Problem was, I didn't want to do the research in the library on Colborne Street where John might see me. Or Caroline, for that matter. It had been hard, but I'd kept my promise to the ghost and not said anything about the wet messages that had appeared in the book.

After school one day, I walked up to the community centre branch of the library to look for information about fishing lures. That library was way bigger than the one on Colborne Street. I walked around confused for a few minutes, not quite sure where to begin. Finally, I decided to ask for some help.

"Do you have any books on old-fashioned fishing lures?" I asked the mousy-looking lady behind the information desk. "I'm trying to find out when they were invented."

I waited while she checked her computer. It felt weird talking to a librarian who wasn't Caroline or her grandmother ... like I was cheating on them by being in another branch.

"Yes, we have a few books that can help you with that," she said, scribbling some numbers down on a yellow Post-it Note. Then, pulling herself to her feet with a barely audible grunt, she led me over in the direction of a long wall of bookshelves. Once I had the right books, it didn't take me long to locate the information I was looking for. Sure enough, like those website had said, fishing lures *did* exist back in the olden days. They were patented around 1890 and before then, they were usually handmade by craftsmen.

Also in the books, I found more pictures of old-fashioned-looking fishing poles and lures. I wondered if any of them looked like the one John wanted me to dig up from the garden. I just wish I knew a bit more about this ghost and why he wanted this lure back so badly. I mean, what did he think he was going to do with it, anyway? Caroline said that ghosts can have a physical presence ... but dead guys can't go fishing, can they?

I went back to the librarian for more books — this time I wanted to find out about ghosts. From the tall stack she collected, I went straight for the one with the creepiest cover. It was called *Paranormal*. After flipping around for a few minutes, I found this inside:

Some spirits are able to gather enough energy to communicate with people and interact with our world. Knocking on walls or windows; opening or slamming doors; moving, throwing, lifting objects; causing things to disappear, even appearing in human form. Cases of spirits having physical contact with people have been reported time and time again throughout history.

I closed the book with a slap as a chill rippled over my skin. Human form? Holy crap! Maybe this dead dude really *was* planning on going fishing! Either way, this definitely explained how he was able to write those wet letters in my textbook. He said his name was John ... but Caroline said there were lots of Johns who'd lived in the house. Which one was the ghost? If only I knew his last name, then maybe I could figure out when he'd been alive. And what had happened to him. And how he had died.

Then I had another idea. Putting the ghost book away, I went back to the information desk for the third time.

"I'm trying to find out if there were any old

newspapers printed in this area back in the 1800s. Can you help me with that?"

The mousy-looking lady frowned. "Well, there were quite a few newspapers coming out of Toronto at the time. But the only local paper would have been *The Richmond Hill Liberal*. That began printing back in … let me see … 1878."

"You wouldn't have any old copies that I can have a look at, would you?"

She let out a high-pitched squeak of a laugh. "Well, no, we don't have the originals, if that's what you're asking. But we do have all of the early newspapers on microfilm. Will that do?"

"Sure … okay, thanks." That was pretty old-school, but I'd take what I could get.

A few minutes later, I was sitting in front of a microfilm reader with the first edition of the *Richmond Hill Liberal* from 1878 on the screen in front of me. I started reading. The newspapers weren't very long back then — only about a page or two. But since I had no idea what I was looking for, I forced myself to go over every article. It didn't take long to figure out that Caroline had been right about one thing — there were a *lot* of guys named John back then. It was like every article mentioned one John or another.

John Lane, John Cook, John Grice, John Martin, John Wright ...

After about an hour, my eyes were going buggy.

What the hell am I doing? This is like searching for a needle in a haystack! I don't even know who I'm looking for!

I glanced up at the clock on the wall. It was 4:39. I decided to give it until 5:00 before quitting. With a tired sigh, I turned back to the microfilm reader. About a minute later, a short article caught my eye. It was from an edition of the newspaper dated September 21, 1889. The headline pulled my heart up into my throat.

Local Boy Still Missing

My pulse hammered in my ears as my eyes took in the rest of the article.

> Residents of the village of Thornhill are still searching for fifteen-year-old John McCallum of 10 Colborne Street, who recently went missing from the area. McCallum was last seen by his cousin, William Bowes in the early morning of August 31st, whilst the pair were fishing in a millpond by the Don River. Accidental drowning is suspected, although both the river and adjacent

pond have been searched and no body recovered. Any persons with information as to the boy's whereabouts are strongly encouraged to contact Robert and Elizabeth McCallum.

By the time I got to the end of the article, all the little hairs on the back of my neck were standing up again. There was not a shred of doubt in my mind that this was it. *I'd found the right John!* The report even mentioned the house on Colborne Street. It *had* to be the same John whose ghost contacted me in the book. The article was accompanied by a small, dark photo. Although it was black and white and pretty grainy ... I could sort of make out John's short, neatly combed hair. When I squinted my eyes, I could kind of see some light reflecting off of his hair, so it might have been blond. But the picture was so smudgy it was hard to tell for sure. The kid seemed to be standing in front of a brick wall. Was this his school photo? He looked young, although the article said that he was fifteen when he disappeared. Just one year younger than me.

I looked at the face of this long-ago boy and suddenly felt a wave of pity push through my insides. The ghost wasn't a woman or a man ... he was a kid like me. If all he wanted was his lure back, that wasn't asking so much, was it?

I sat back in the chair, staring at the grainy photograph on the screen in front of me. Getting official permission was taking way too long. It was the end of October ... the ground would start to freeze in another month. I didn't want to wait until next spring to help this poor kid get his lure back.

Yeah, I was going to have to take matters into my own hands.

17 – John

Like an angry bull, I charged through the thick mud and seized William's fishing pole.

"You thief!" My voice was so laden with fury that I scared myself with the sound. "Give me back my lure!"

For a brief second, William's brown eyes widened in shock. Clearly, he hadn't expected a fight from me. But an instant later, they narrowed back into dark slits. A smirk played upon his lips. "Calm yourself, Cousin," he replied, pulling the pole away from my grabbing hands. "All I want is one more chance to catch Sir John A. before I leave for Kingston. Then I'll return your precious lure."

But I refused to release the pole. It was as if it had been bonded to my fingers. "Give it to me," I growled. "It's my lure! I won't let you use it!"

The smirk disappeared from William's countenance, leaving a dark scowl in its place. "Stubborn
fool!" he taunted. Then, hurling his palm against my
chest, he shoved me roughly to the ground. I lay frozen there for a moment, catching the breath that had
been knocked from my lungs and silently gathering
my strength. There, on the muddy bank of the pond, I
thought about all the years of mischief and misery I'd
had to endure at my cousin's hands. In a few hours,
he would be leaving to embark upon the next phase of
his life. The realization poured over me like a bucket
of cold water: this was to be our final confrontation.

And I would *not* lose to him again.

The sound of William's snickering pulled me back
to the moment. "Now run along home to Mama, little boy," I heard him chortle as he turned back in the
direction of the pond.

A moment later, the tip of William's fishing pole bent
down in a quick, jerking motion. "I've got something!"
he cried out, forgetting all about me as he began to
reel in his line. And in the next instant, something happened that had never happened before. Suddenly, I felt
an enormous, irrepressible, all-consuming feeling of
anger boil up inside my chest. The anger was red, hot,
and urgent. It spread up and down my limbs like a disease until every muscle was seized with rage. It felt as

if a demon had taken over my body. My hands curled into fists and my teeth clenched against each other like a grinding mill. With a savage cry, I leapt up from the ground, grabbed William by the shirt, and pulled him backwards. He fell upon his backside with a loud thud. The force of the fall must have surprised him, for the fishing pole flew back from his hands onto the muddy bank behind us. There it lay, free for the taking. But I was so consumed with anger that I didn't even think to retrieve it. Looking back on that day, as I have so many times over the past century, I can honestly report that in the heat of my anger, I had completely forgotten about the lure. At that point, all I wanted was to hurt William. To beat him down, even the score, and force him to surrender by any means possible.

This was my state of mind when I jumped to my feet and pulled my leg back to deliver a vicious kick to my rival's ribcage. But William was faster than I had anticipated. Roaring with fury, he caught my foot in mid-air and pulled me back down into the mud. My shoulder took the brunt of my weight as I fell to the ground. I heard something snap but, so consumed as I was with the fight, I paid little heed to what it might be.

Hurt ... maim ... hit ... kick ... destroy.

These were the thoughts that were beating through my brain.

A blow fell upon my face. And then another. My nose swelled with a wet heat that I knew must have been my own blood. But I was entirely too numb with rage to feel the pain. William was certainly heavier and stronger, but I was angrier, which evened our battle somewhat. "Give up, you puny runt!" he growled, landing another blow across my face. Instead of replying, I threw my head mightily forward against William's. The sound of our skulls connecting was a sickening crack, like a dried stick being snapped in two. Now it was William's blood that was flowing, which gave me more satisfaction than I can properly describe.

Had there been anybody passing by the pond at that early hour, they might have surmised that a fight was taking place between two large, feral animals. By that point, William and I were entirely covered in mud and filth and blood and snarling at one another like a couple of wild boars. The fishing pole lay on the ground behind us, forgotten while we scuffled on the bank of the pond.

Suddenly, I heard William call out.

"Stop! It's still on the line!"

I turned my bloody head in the direction of his gaze to see William's fishing pole flying across the bank, as if being dragged by an invisible hand. If I hadn't known better, I might have thought it was being transported by a ghost.

"It's Sir John A.!" hollered William, trying to wrest himself free from my grip. Surprised by the moving pole, I released my hold on him. Whether it was Sir John A. or some other fish, I never was able to discern. But it was clear from the speed the pole was travelling through the mud that whatever was caught on the other end of the line must have been a creature quite big and strong.

"Come back!" William howled. The pole was just moments away from falling into the pond. We dove in unison to catch it. Mud splattered like an outbreak of measles across my face and I squeezed my lids shut to keep my eyes safe from the filth. Groping blindly for the runaway pole, I felt a great flash of triumph when my fingers found it and locked themselves around the narrow length of wood in a death grip. But William's hands were fast, too. An instant later, my triumph faded away as I felt him seize the pole with all his strength and pull hard. I held fast and pulled back as the ire in my belly flared up again. The battle between cousins continued, both of us doggedly determined to cheat the other one out of this final victory.

"Let go!" William barked in my face. His nostrils were flaring furiously.

"No, you let go!" I grunted back. Together, we staggered back and forth on the shoreline like a pair of demented dancers, each of us refusing to give up the lead. Beside us, a startled flock of geese took flight over the water, honking loudly in outrage as they soared over our heads. Envy pricked at my heart as I watched their graceful escape. My energy was flagging. More than anything, I wanted to drop the fishing pole and fly away with those geese. The cloud of numbness was beginning to rise off me like the mist from the water. And that's when the hurt began to set in. Suddenly, I could feel the intense pain of my broken nose, the ache of my sore limbs, the throbbing of my fractured shoulder. That's when I knew I'd had enough. Gathering every bit of strength from my exhausted muscles, I yanked on the fishing pole for the final time. It flew from William's grasp.

I've won.

This was my only thought as I stumbled backward from the force of my exertion. My shoes slipped on the muddy bank and in one fluid motion, with the fishing pole still clenched in my hands, I fell right over the edge of the precipice.

Into the pond I landed with a sinister splash.

The mill pond was surprisingly cold that late August morning ... as if the warmth of the summer had been sucked from its depths overnight. Although shocked by the chilly water, fear didn't claim my mood immediately, for I stupidly thought it would be a simple task to pull myself back up onto the bank. Before I could catch my balance, however, I felt my body being swallowed up as the bottom of the pond sunk beneath my feet like quicksand. Terror quickly set in as the mud devoured my feet, my shins, my knees. I tried to raise myself out before the rest of my body was overcome by the pond, but my feet were stuck fast.

"Help!" I managed to cry before my face was dragged down beneath the waterline. William scrambled to the edge of the bank and stretched his hand out to pull me back. "Clumsy fool," he chided, although the expression on his countenance was tight with worry. His fingers hovered over the water, a few inches out of my grasp. "Come closer and I'll pull you out. Then I can finish you off properly."

Although I desperately wanted to be reassured by William's seeming lack of concern for me, his act was not convincing in the slightest. As good a liar as my cousin had proven himself to be over the years, he simply wasn't able to hide the dark streak of terror flashing across his features. And his voice shook with the imminent peril of my situation.

"Reach, John …" he begged, stretching his long body out onto the bank to support my weight "Just a bit closer and I'll have you."

I leaned my waterlogged body toward William's outstretched hand.

"Almost there … just a bit farther," he urged.

A moment later, the tips of my fingers brushed William's, filling my heart with a slight gasp of hope. Just another inch or two and my hand would be in his. In my panic to reach him, I pulled on my stuck feet with all my strength, aware that my life depended on taking one more step. But as only one foot came loose from the mud, I lost my balance and fell sideways down into the pond. I was in the midst of screaming when my head went under the surface. My mouth, my ears, my nose were suddenly filled with brown water as my head plunged into the pond. And as much as I tried to cough the murky liquid out, more kept spilling in. I felt something long and sharp snaking its way around my ankles, binding them tightly, cutting into my skin. I tried to kick my legs free, but that just made it worse. My head spun with panic as I lost all sense of direction. Which way was up? Could William still see me even though I couldn't see him? I opened my eyes, but the pond was so cloudy from my flailing that I couldn't see anything. I tried waving my hands to signal my location, but my exhausted muscles and fractured shoulder prevented me from breaking the surface. Of course, it didn't help that my ankles were still mysteriously bound, anchoring me to the bottom of the pond.

It was oddly silent down there. Under the weight of the water, I could only move at a snail's pace. Every time I attempted to scream, another mouthful of water poured into me and burned a path down my throat. It only took a few seconds for the fire in my throat to spread to my chest. My lungs felt like they were burning for air and the fire only intensified with every missed breath. Panic seized my pounding heart as I realized the inescapable truth of the situation.

I was drowning.

Once I gave up the struggle, the end of my life was surprisingly peaceful. Quite the opposite of how you might imagine a death scene. There were no screams, no sobs, no desperate last-moment supplications to the Lord above ... just the sound of water swishing over my ears and the beat of my racing heart banging against my ribs. When I saw the last bubble of air escape my lungs and rise up in front of my face, I knew it was over. At that moment, I gave up fighting and allowed my arms to hang limply in the water. A beautiful sensation of floating took over as I let the cold water wrap around my body like an icy blanket.

A gentle, fluid embrace.

The softest one I was to ever know.

And then, in the last moment of my life, I looked toward the heavens. Some distance above me, I thought I could see the blurred silhouette of William's head against the grey morning sky. He was bent over the water, searching the muddy depths for my face.

And then I was gone.

18 — Max

I waited until I was sure my parents were asleep before sneaking out of my room. It was twenty minutes past midnight when I crept down the stairs as silently as my big feet would allow and stole out into the late October night. Luckily I didn't have far to go, because the sight of me with the shovel in my hand and my hood pulled down low over my face would have raised red flags in even the most trusting of passersby. Strangely enough, if it was just one day later on the calendar my ghoulish appearance probably wouldn't lift a single eyebrow. The next night was Halloween, after all. For the past week, most of the houses in this residential neighbourhood have been getting into full 'fright' mode. On my way to the library, I passed gang after gang of decorative monsters, witches, and bloody corpses. And vampires. Seems like there were way more vampires than usual this year.

I shivered as I skulked down the street toward the library, wishing I'd thought to bring along a pair of gloves. It was cold outside. There would be a frost tonight, for sure. My shoes kicked through the river of dried leaves that had collected on the sidewalk, crunching and crackling with every step.

When I got to 10 Colborne Street, I paused for a moment in the driveway and stared up at the second-storey window, looking for the figure of the shadowy grey lady.

If I see her, it'll be a sign ... no, a warning. A warning to forget this crazy scheme and go home to bed.

I waited for a full minute, half hoping she'd appear and relieve me of my responsibilities. The white building seemed to glow against the backdrop of the night sky. But the windows remained dark and empty. With a sigh, I balanced the long shovel handle over my right shoulder and trudged up the garden path toward the spot where John had drawn the X in the dirt almost two weeks ago. You'd think I would be a bit more excited to finally be digging up that lure for him. But I wasn't at all. Somewhere in the deepest pit of my stomach, a bad feeling was beginning to grow — a feeling urging me to walk away from the library and not look back.

Lure

But I couldn't do it. For some reason, the pull of this place was stronger tonight than it had ever been before. There was no turning back now.

I snuck around to the side of the building, looking for the spot behind the balsams where John had marked the X. It was dark back there away from the dim light of the streetlamps, like the gardens had been wrapped in a thick layer of shadow. Damn, I should have brought a flashlight, too! For the second time in a matter of minutes, I considered turning around and going home. The thought was tempting. Maybe I could try to sneak out here another night when I was better prepared. This job would definitely go easier with the proper equipment. But I'd made a promise to John — I was going to get his lure back. The ground would start to freeze soon. It was now or never.

Now ... the maple tree beside me whispered, as a breeze shook the last of its red leaves to the ground. Yes ... *now*, my heart silently agreed.

Lifting the shovel up in the air, I plunged the sharp end into the dirt with a gritty thump. I did that three more times until the surface of the cold ground was broken up nicely. And then I started to dig. But before the hole was even a foot deep, the sound of a siren screaming somewhere in the background froze my arms with fear.

Had someone seen me sneak back here with the shovel? Had they called the police? I went over the list of criminal activities I was in the midst of committing. Trespassing, destruction of property, defacing an historic building ... oh crap, this was so bad! I clung to the metal handle of the shovel, trying to decipher whether the siren was getting nearer or farther away. Despite the cold night air, my entire body was breaking out into a nervous sweat. A few seconds later, my heart stopped racing as I heard the siren fade away into the distance. Only when it had completely disappeared into the dark night did I wipe my sweaty palms off on my jeans and start to dig again.

With every shovel full of dirt I hoisted from the hole, the bad feeling in the pit of my stomach got stronger and stronger. What exactly did I think I was doing out here in the middle of the night? Why exactly was I carrying out the bidding of a ghost? I must be certifiably crazy! Just a few weeks ago, I didn't even believe in ghosts! And now suddenly I'd become a gofer for a teenage phantom with a fishing obsession? If someone found me out here, I'd be in all kinds of trouble. And what would I say to defend myself if that happened?

Sorry Officer, but I'm digging up the heritage garden because a soggy book told me to do it.

Yeah, right! Nobody in their right mind would believe me! They'd lock me up in an asylum and throw away the key! And I wouldn't even blame them. And what about my parents? They'd ground me for life if they knew what I was doing!

But as ridiculous as I knew this whole scheme was, I kept right on digging. Even though my stomach felt like it was going to erupt with nerves. Trickles of sweat ran down my nose and dripped into the hole below me. My muscles started to protest with pain as the hole slowly grew bigger. How deep down was I going to have to dig for this thing? A part of me (the rational part) doubted I was going to find something down there, anyway. And even if there was a lure buried in this garden, what was I going to do when I found it? How exactly was I going to give it back to John? He was a ghost, after all.

Yeah, this was without a doubt the stupidest thing I'd ever done. Caroline would probably never talk to me again if she knew what I was doing out here. I closed my eyes and pictured her face, her hair, her eyes. I was most likely ruining whatever slim chance I might have with her by doing this.

And then, just as that last thought was forming in my head, the shovel hit something hard.

Crack!

The aching muscles in my back and arms twitched with relief at the sound. My eyes flew open. *Finally, this must be it!* Immediately, I eased up on the shovel and dug with much more care. Now that I'd worked so hard to find this thing, I didn't want to break it. It was probably fragile, like any antique would be. Especially one that had been buried underground for a century, or maybe even more.

After another harsh-sounding crack, I put down the shovel and peered into the hole. But it was so dark, I couldn't see anything. Not even my freezing bare hands rubbing together for warmth in front of me. *That flashlight would have been really useful right now*, I thought, kneeling to get a closer look at what was down there. But there was no use. I was blind back there in the dense shadows.

Stretching myself out on the ground, I reached as far as I could into the hole. Luckily, my arms are long, so I could just make contact with the object. I ran my fingers over it, trying to gauge its size and shape. It felt like a large, stone container ... or maybe it was carved out of wood. It was hard to tell just by the feel of it because it was so caked with dirt. It was definitely roundish, but it had two large openings on the top the size of quarters. I dug around the edges of the object, trying to loosen it from the soil. When it was finally free from the ground, I yanked it up from the dark depths of the hole. I was so eager to finally have a look at this thing that John wanted returned so badly.

But what I pulled from that cold, black earth wasn't a lure at all. And it wasn't a round, wooden box, either. What I pulled from the hole turned my blood to ice the instant I realized what I was holding in my hands. Worms twisting and flailing out from every socket, its horrifying grimace was practically glowing in the dark.

Flinging the thing back down to the ground, I closed my eyes and began screaming at the top of my voice, not caring who heard me. Not caring if I woke up the entire neighbourhood. Not caring if someone called the police. And then I tore out of that garden and raced back home like I was being chased by the devil himself.

Because what I'd dug up from that hole in the middle of the night was the most terrifying, shocking, grotesque thing I'd ever had the misfortune of seeing in my entire life.

It was … as you've probably guessed by now … a human skull.

19 – John

William stretched out on the muddy bank, flattening his body like a large slab of stone. Then he reached his shaking hand as far into the water as possible without falling into the pond himself.

"John! John!" He was screaming my name over and over, as if trying to salvage the severed connection between us. When he saw my limp arm floating near the surface he grabbed onto it with both hands and pulled mightily. The mud loosened its grip on my feet and my heavy, waterlogged corpse was laboriously heaved out of the water and laid out on the shore. A thin length of white fishing line was still tangled around my ankles, like a spider web wrapped around its prey. The dripping lure dangled ridiculously from the hem of my pants.

Lure

How ironic that I'd been caught by the line while Sir John A. had managed to escape.

However, in his panic, William took no notice of this. "Wake up, John!" my cousin commanded. But by that point, it was too late. My spirit had flown from its human shell and was already watching from the top of the old, bent willow tree behind us.

Of course, William didn't know that. Tearing open my soaked shirt, he pushed and thumped on my chest like a maniac. Was he trying to force the water from my lungs or restart my stalled heart? I'll never know the answer. When he was done hitting me, he picked me up by the shoulders and shook me like rag doll.

"Come now, John! Don't do this!" he shrieked. "Open your eyes!"

My head flopped ridiculously back and forth. Droplets of water sprayed from my hair in all directions, like a dog just come in from the rain. But William's dim-witted efforts to revive me were fruitless. There was no trace of life left in my body to salvage. When my cousin finally realized this truth, he grasped my sodden hand between his and began to weep.

If my heart were still beating, it would most certainly have been touched.

William sobbed hysterically beside my lifeless body for several minutes, until the sound of the milkman's horse trotting up the dirt road caused him to stop crying and look up. I can only guess that the notion of a witness to the tragic scene on the shores of the mill pond is what brought him back to his senses. The sky was now a light shade of grey. Daybreak was approaching and the rest of the village would soon be awake. What was William going to tell them? How was he going to explain my death? I was morbidly fascinated to find out.

Keeping very still, William crouched down behind the reeds and waited for the milkman to pass. As soon as he and his horse were out of sight, William hoisted my limp body into his arms and began to carry me back through the mist-covered fields ... back to the house at 10 Colborne Street. My spirit followed close behind like a cool, dark shadow.

Looking back, I think my cousin must have entered a state of shock at that point, for he was shaking uncontrollably, his skin had turned a sickening shade of green, and he was mumbling to my dead body, as if the two of us were engaged in a real conversation. Knowing this, perhaps you'll judge his actions less harshly. That will be your decision. As for me, I will continue to damn his soul to eternal hellfire for what he was about to do.

"Dear Lord, how am I going to face Aunt Elizabeth? How shall I tell her that you're dead? Her only child?

It will surely kill her, too. And Uncle Robert? What will he say? Will he hold me responsible for your death because I lured you out to the pond?"

Guilt quickly changed to fear as his rambling thoughts turned to his soft, blue-eyed fiancée and the life they were planning together.

"What will Martha think of all this? Will she still want to marry me?" He looked down at my battered face, my bent nose, my bloated, unblinking eyes. And then he gasped audibly at the horrible notion forming in his head.

"Good God! What if they accuse me of killing you, John?" he whispered into my unhearing ears. "There were no witnesses, after all, to attest that it was an accident. What if they try to hold me responsible for your death?"

And then he paused, as if hoping I might possibly give him an answer. We were just coming up behind the house at that point and the sky was changing from grey to white. A bird twittered a morning song from a nearby tree. Soon the rest of the village would be awake and William would have to explain what had happened. He skulked through the opening in the fence outside our home and laid my body down next to Mother's rose garden. His head whipped around in all directions, as if searching for a solution to his ghastly dilemma. In just a few more minutes, his fate would be laid out for others to decide.

"Who will believe me if I tell the truth?" he moaned under his breath.

Fresh tears streamed down his cheeks as he struggled to decide his next move. Did I mention before that my cousin had reclaimed his senses? Surely, it was a fleeting recovery. For if I didn't know William so well, I would have thought him a madman by his appearance as we hid in the shadow of the house, waiting for daybreak. His clothes and face were still covered in mud, the cut on his forehead where I'd butted him was caked with dried blood, his eyes were wild with fear, and his teeth were chattering violently. He was frightening to behold.

And perhaps he did go mad that morning, for certainly his next decision was not that of a rational man. There, amidst Mother's beloved roses, arrived the pivotal moment in William's life. His soul was balancing on the point of a deadly knife.

Now, if William had had the courage to do the right thing, my spirit would have been able to rest and this would have been the end of my story. But in the early rays of dawn on that late August morning, my cousin made an appalling decision ... a treacherous decision. A decision that stole away my rights to a peaceful demise. As the first fiery rays of sunlight broke across the sky, William chose to take the path of deceit. And his deceit has left my spirit unsettled for all these years.

With only minutes to go before my parents would be rising from their beds, William ran to the barn to retrieve Father's shovel. And then he dug a hasty grave and buried me in the garden at the side of the house.

"I'm sorry, John," he moaned, lowering me down into the wet, black earth. At least he'd done me the decency of closing my eyes to keep the worms out. "I'll tell them you stayed on at the pond while I returned to pack my bags. I'll tell them you wouldn't listen when I begged you to come … that you hit my head when I tried to drag you home. I'll tell them you were threatening to run away so you wouldn't have to work in the forge anymore. Oh God, forgive me, John!"

While the rooster at the neighbouring red cottage announced the start of the day, William finished covering me up with dirt and wilted flowers. And with that, the thick curtain of darkness fell over me and I disappeared.

But of course, as you already know, my restless spirit remained.

20 — Max

The very next day on the morning of Halloween, Caroline's beloved garden was torn apart by a bulldozer. It didn't take long for the rest of the skeleton to be found. One by one, they pulled the dirt-encrusted bones from the earth. I was there, watching in horror from the sidewalk. The scene in front of me made my stomach churn — but I couldn't help myself. It was like an awful accident you couldn't pry your eyes away from.

When the bulldozer was done, the men and women with the masks and plastic gloves moved in to gather up the remains. They collected the pieces in special bags and then dug around some more to make sure there weren't any other bodies down there. But I didn't wait around to watch that part. As I was leaving, I heard someone say it would take weeks for the DNA tests to come back to determine the age and sex of the person whose skull I'd held in my hands.

I didn't need to wait that long for the answer. I knew who those bones belonged to.

After that day, I didn't go back to the library again. I was way too ashamed to face Caroline after what I'd done. Even though she'd been standing just a few feet away during the excavation, she wouldn't even look at me. Maybe it was because she was mad at me. Or maybe it was because she was too busy crying. She and Nana had been watching together, both of their faces soaked with tears at the sight of their treasured antique garden getting ripped apart. I knew she hated me for ruining it. And for sneaking around behind her back and lying to her.

And the thing was ... I really couldn't blame her one bit.

Weeks went by and I buried myself in schoolwork, trying my hardest to forget I'd ever known her. But it didn't work. Little bits and pieces of her were constantly creeping in and out of my thoughts: her voice, her smell, her dimples, her eyes. It was like I had a disease and there was no cure for it.

Every day on my way to school I passed by Colborne Street with my chin tucked into my neck and my eyes glued to my shoes. I didn't even want to see the library in case the place was trying to suck me back in. The pull of it was still there, but not nearly as strong as before. I guess regret and shame are more powerful emotions than temptation.

But man, I missed Caroline. *Badly*. And in a weird way, I even missed John. I wondered how he ended up buried in an unmarked grave. If there had ever been a fishing lure at all. Why he chose me to find his body. And why he tricked me into digging him up like that? Did he really drown all those years ago? Or had someone killed him?

I had to accept the fact that I'd probably never know those answers. The only thing I knew for sure was that John was desperate to be found — for people to see him and know he was there. I guess it was kind of like how I'd been so desperate for people to see me when I first started coming to the library. Lying in an unmarked grave was like being invisible forever ... like you'd never even existed. It must have been the worst feeling in the world. I can only guess that John needed to find someone he could trust to help him ... someone who understood his desperation enough to rescue him from it. And that's probably why he chose to contact me. Because I was invisible, too.

Lure

Sorry, I *used* to be invisible. Since the night I dug up the skull, all that's changed. The police have been lining up to interview me and so have all the local newspapers and TV stations. I've had dozens of ghost hunters and psychics calling me, wanting to hear my story. And absolutely every kid at my school suddenly knew my name. For two weeks straight, I couldn't walk down the hall without somebody stopping me to ask about the body in the garden and the ghost in the library and how the two were connected.

But in the end, it was really Caroline who had changed everything around for me. She'd seen me better than anyone. She'd stepped up and been my friend when nobody else would do it. And I'd gone and ruined it all.

I was miserable without her.

And then, one afternoon in early December, there was a knock at my front door. I'd come home from school and had just poured myself a bowl of cereal and flipped on the TV. When I looked through the peephole and saw who was standing on the front porch, I almost stopped breathing. It took me a full minute to build up the nerve to open the door. *Was she here to yell at me? Tell me how much she hated my guts?* I braced myself for the worst as I pulled open the door. The instant I did, the old hammer was swinging into my stomach and I almost slammed it shut again. She was so pretty, I could barely stand to look at her. A blue wool cap covered most of her hair except for a few golden pieces that had come loose around her face. And her cheeks and nose were pink from the wintry air. Peanut was there, too, faithfully standing guard at her feet. I don't know how it was possible, but Caroline's blue eyes looked sadder than the little pug's.

"How did you find out where I live?" I blurted. I was so shocked, I didn't even say hi which I guess was kind of rude. But honestly, I just was too freaked out to give a rat's ass about manners.

She looked surprised by my question. "I-I went to your school and asked the secretary for your address."

"And they gave it to you? I don't think they're supposed to do that."

"Yeah, well … it's amazing the kind of information you can get your hands on when you flash an official-looking form."

"What are you talking about?" I demanded, looking at her like she was speaking a foreign language. My words were coming out a lot harsher than I wanted, but I couldn't help it. "What form?"

"This one." Her voice was small as she held out a folded piece of white paper. "It's the permission form for you to work on the garden. Little late, I guess …"

Lure

I can't believe she's here, outside my house after all these weeks and we're talking about forms!

I took the paper from her and scanned my eyes down the page. *Maxwell Green is hereby granted permission to work in the heritage garden at 10 Colborne Street, which is protected ... blah blah blah.* It had been signed by the mayor of Markham and someone from the Thornhill Public Library that I'd never heard of before.

"Who's Martha Henry Reid?" I asked, pointing to the second signature.

She laughed at that. But it was a sad, hollow laugh. "That's Nana."

"Your nana's middle name is *Henry*?"

"It's a family name. She was named after ... um, her mother."

"Okay, well, thanks for bringing this over," I said folding the paper back up. "But it's too late in the year for any more gardening. And, well ... I was kind of lying about that, anyway. The fact is I just wanted to dig around without getting in trouble. Sorry I wasn't honest with you."

She nodded, but didn't say anything as she tucked the form back into her purse. Her breath was coming out in thin white clouds and I could see that she was shivering from the cold, despite her hat and big puffy coat. If it was anybody else freezing on my doorstep, I'd invite them to come in where it was warmer. But my stomach was still getting battered by having her so close. I wanted to get this over with as fast as possible. Since I'd just confessed to one lie, I figured I might as well come clean about the rest of them. She hated me, anyway, so it didn't matter at this point. *Right?*

"So, look ..." I said, letting out a long deep breath. "... I guess I should tell you that I also lied about my age. I'm actually sixteen ... not seventeen."

The muscles in her face tightened, like she was trying to hold something back. Was she pissed off at me for lying? Or at herself for wasting so much time on a kid? Why wasn't she saying anything? Man, she must *really* hate me. I bit the inside of my cheek so hard, I tasted blood. That's how nervous I was.

"And I'm a sophomore in high school, not a senior ..." I continued, digging my hole even deeper.

A gust of wind blew across the porch, sending the first tiny snowflakes of the year whipping through the air. Peanut licked his lips and whined softly. After a few more seconds dragged by with no reply, I figured Caroline's thoughts were pretty clear. It was time to put her out of her misery.

"So, thanks for coming. I guess I'll see you around ..."

Lure

Just as I was about to swing the door shut, she took a small step forward and reached out to stop me. "No, don't. Please. I ... I lied to you, too, Max."

She'd been lying, too? About what? My mind started spinning in frantic circles. "W-what do you mean?"

Her eyes dropped to the floor and her pretty lips turned down into a sad pout. "God, there's just so much you don't know. I'm not even sure how to begin ..." she closed her eyes as her words trailed off, "... I'm not the age I told you I was, either. You'd never believe me if I told you how old I truly am. And my name's not really Caroline."

My mouth fell open with shock. "What did you say?"

That's when she started to cry. I stood there like a complete idiot, not knowing what to say or do. Why had she lied about her name? And why was she crying? I didn't understand any of this. I was aching to comfort her, but had no idea how. After a long moment, she lifted her eyes back to mine. They were as blue as a cloudless sky and filled with tears. "I ... I was just trying to help bring you into the library," she whispered, her voice shattered like broken glass. "I didn't expect these feelings. Dear God, it's been so long since I felt this way. And then when you stopped coming, I felt like dying all over again. I ... I guess I just needed to see you one more time."

I couldn't believe what I was hearing. "What are you talking about? I ... I thought you hated me."

"Hated you?" she let out a wry laugh. "No, just the opposite. I liked you. I still like you ... a lot." Her chin was beginning to quiver, like she was about to start sobbing again. If a brick had fallen on my head at that moment, I probably wouldn't have felt it. How could I have been so wrong about everything?

And then out of the corner of my eye, I saw a grey minivan pull up in the driveway. It was my mom. *Crap! I'm not ready for this conversation to end yet.* Reaching behind me, I yanked my jacket down from the coat rack.

"Honestly, I don't care about the lies. I don't care what your real name is or how old you are. I just want to be with you ... but my mom's here." I threw my arms through the sleeves. "If we stay, she won't leave us alone. So maybe we can go somewhere else to talk for a while?"

She shook her head sadly. "No, I can't do that. I really have to go. I just came here to see you one last time ... and to give you this."

Reaching into her purse, she pulled out a little, flat box. "After they finished digging around the rest of the garden, they found this not far from the ... you know, the bones. They offered it to the library, but Nana didn't want it. So I figured it would be all right if I gave it to you."

"What is it?" I asked, highly aware of my mother watching us from the driveway. By the shocked look on her face, I was sure she was dying to find out the identity of the pretty blonde on her front porch.

"No, please don't open it yet ... wait till after I go."

I shook my head. "What? Where are you going?"

Her eyes looked like they were melting with sadness. "Far away," she whispered, wiping a stray tear out of the corner of her eye. "But there's something I've been dying to do ... something I've been thinking about since the day we met." A pair of blood-red roses were blooming across her pale cheeks.

"What is it?"

Rising up on her toes, she brushed her lips against mine, gentle as a feather. I was too stunned to do anything else except stand there like a statue and breathe in her awesome smell. She was so incredibly soft. Her lips, her mouth, her skin ... so soft, but so icy cold at the same time. I put my arms around her and pressed my hands to the curve of her back. I wanted it to last forever — but the kiss was over before it had barely begun.

"Goodbye, Max," she whispered into my lips. *Goodbye?* I opened my eyes and she was gone. Disappeared.

What just happened? Where did she go so fast?

A sudden frigid gust of wind surged across the porch, stirring up a cloud of snowflakes. I peered through the flurry, searching for Caroline — but there was just Peanut whining at my feet and my mother's angry face charging up the driveway toward me.

"Max! Why are you standing there with the door open, letting all the heat out of the house? Why is there a dog on our porch? You know I'm allergic! And did I just see you talking to yourself? Honestly, your father and I are having a hard time understanding your behaviour these days! You're not doing drugs, are you? Is that what's in that box?"

Ignoring my mother's questions, I glanced down and saw that I was still holding the box Caroline had given me. With trembling fingers, I lifted the lid. What I saw inside made me choke on my own breath. There, nestled on a ball of white cotton was a small, silver gadget, with four little wings sticking out and a withered orange feather attached to the end.

The lure.

21 — John

My cousin William went on to marry Martha Henry a few months later and open up his own blacksmith shop, exactly as planned. Although nobody remotely suspected that he might have had a hand in my disappearance, the guilt he felt over what he had done ate away at his conscience like a cancerous mass. Just five years into their marriage, the young couple succumbed to a deadly epidemic of typhus that was winding its way through Kingston. On his deathbed, William unburdened his soul and confessed his crime to his pretty wife, who was only days away from her own death. They left behind a young daughter, who'd inherited her mother's sky-blue eyes along with her name.

It brought me a surprising amount of grief to see William and Martha meet such a tragic end.

As for my parents, they waited over a year for me to return home. My mother spent most of that time crying, moaning, calling out my name, and praying for my safe deliverance from whatever dark forces might have led to our separation. My father, as you might imagine, tried his best to convince Mother to begin the grieving process so that she might forget about me and move ahead with her life. It took many months, but finally my mother stopped watching at the parlour window for my face to emerge outside. She stopped listening for my footsteps coming up the front walk. She accepted that I was gone. And by the first anniversary of my mysterious disappearance, Mother donned her black veil and mourning dress and began to pray for my everlasting soul.

For she knew in her heart that I would never have willingly left her without saying goodbye. After so much time had passed, my absence could only be explained in one horrifying way. Tragically, however, she had no way to prove that I was deceased. And so my dear mother was forced to mourn alone.

In 1890, she agreed to let Father move them to another house. But she never gave up the hope that she would see me again one day — even if that meant reconnecting with my soul in the afterlife. Desperate to uncover the truth about what had happened to me, she brought in a medium and conducted a séance one afternoon when Father was away working in the forge. I watched the whole thing and tried in every possible manner to send a message to let her know what had happened to me. But the veil of darkness that had come over me was so heavy and dense; I could simply not get past it.

Not until now, that is. Not until a boy came along whose emotions mirrored my own so well that a small window slid open in the darkness and allowed a bit of me to slip through to reach him. Lured in, as you have guessed, by the ghost of a pretty young woman who desperately wanted to help right a husband's tragic wrong.

Last week, my remains were laid to rest in a proper grave in the Thornhill Community Cemetery on Church Lane, just a short walk away from 10 Colborne Street. The plot was marked with a simple, grey marble headstone. Although it doesn't bear my name, the stone is engraved with a prayer and that satisfies me. For now, everyone who passes by will be aware of a young life that came and went. And perhaps now that I have been discovered, my dear mother will be able to see me. And both of our spirits will find peace. For that is all I ever wanted, really.

That is all one can ever hope for in this world.

Afterword

The Thornhill Village Public Library at 10 Colborne Street in Markham, Ontario, is a real place. Originally built as a home in 1851, many people believe the building to be haunted. Most of the supernatural occurrences listed in this book are documented incidents that have been reported by both staff and visitors of the library over the past several decades.

The story connecting these supernatural events, however, is completely a product of my imagination, as are the characters you have met in this book.

If you are in the Toronto area and are interested in learning more, you can visit the library (which is a designated historic building), as well as the impressive heritage garden surrounding the property.

It's a great place to read, reflect, and become inspired.

Acknowledgements

This story came to life in the late summer of 2009 with a flash of inspiration and a feverish four weeks of non-stop writing. But the words circling through my head would never have turned into a book without the incredible support of some very wonderful people.

First and foremost, I'd like to thank Jonah and Dahlia for giving up their mom to the muse and putting up with the distracted, forgetful lady who took her place for four weeks.

Forever love to Jordy, for picking up all the pieces and faithfully holding things together while I retreated from the world to write. I couldn't do any of this without you.

Love and thanks to Shirley Pape, whose wisdom and advice is a treasure I am finally old enough to fully appreciate.

Deborah Kerbel

Thanks to my legion of trusted readers; Gordon Pape, Kim, Kendra, and Michael Pape-Green, Sharon Jones, and Shayna Avinoam for their honesty and insights.

Sincere thanks to Kathy Pless for giving me the "ghost tour" and Diane Macklin for granting me access to the off-limits section of the Thornhill Village Library.

Thanks to Adam Birrell and James Broughton, who easily answered all of the trickiest historical questions and opened the doors to the Thornhill Archives for me.

Huge thanks to the Ontario Arts Council for their generous support through the Writers' Reserve Program.

And, as always, I'd like to thank Margaret Hart and the amazingly hard-working team at Dundurn Press, especially Kirk Howard, Michael Carroll, Shannon Whibbs, Margaret Bryant, Karen McMullin, Ashleigh Gardner, Jennifer Scott, and Courtney Horner for their endless enthusiasm and continued support.

Also by Deborah Kerbel

Mackenzie, Lost and Found
978-1-55002-852-2 / $12.99

Nothing prepares fifteen-year-old Mackenzie Hill for the bombshell announcement that her and her dad, alone since the death of her mother a year ago, are moving to Jerusalem. The adjustment from life in Canada to life in Israel is dramatic, though it's eased somewhat by a new friend at school. But the biggest shock of all comes when Mackenzie faces the wrath of her new friends, new community, and even her own father after she begins dating a Muslim boy.

Girl on the Other Side
978-1-55488-443-8 / $12.99

Tabby Freeman and Lora Froggett go to the same school, but they live in totally opposite worlds. Tabby is rich, pretty, and the most popular girl in her class. On the other side, Lora is smart, timid, and the constant target of bullies. Despite their differences, Tabby and Lora have something in common — they're both harbouring dark secrets and a lot of pain. Although they've never been friends, a series of strange events causes their lives to crash together in ways neither could have ever imagined. And when the dust finally settles and all their secrets are forced out into the light, will the girls be saved ... or destroyed?

Available at your favourite bookseller.

DUNDURN PRESS
www.dundurn.com

What did you think of this book?

Visit www.dundurn.com
for reviews, videos, updates, and more!